FOR MORE MISS RIDDELL

To be kept up-to-date with future Miss Riddell's Cozy Mysteries, sign up for my newsletter here.

And to pre-order the next book, follow this link: Girl in a Gazebo

MISS RIDDELL'S PARANORMAL MYSTERY

AN AMATEUR FEMALE SLEUTH HISTORICAL COZY MYSTERY

P.C. JAMES

A NOTE TO THE READER:

This is a very strange story in that the normal events it describes are fiction, made up by the author, and therefore not real. The paranormal events in the story, however, are *not* fiction, being only *described* by the author, to the best of his ability, and they were very definitely real. In this story, the natural way of fiction and reality is reversed. I explain further at the end.

1

LITHGOW, NEW SOUTH WALES, AUSTRALIA – 1978

THE JOURNEY UP from Sydney airport had felt as tiring as the twenty-four hours of flying and flight changes from London had been. The company car on the drive through Sydney's growing suburbs and into the Blue Mountains was air-conditioned, thankfully, for it was way too hot for someone of Pauline's British background. Now, indoors with the motel air-conditioning running, she was beginning to unwind.

She'd flown out to Australia a few days early to take up a temporary posting of six months. The job was at the Australian subsidiary where she'd done an audit only three months before. It was that audit which had led to the local finance director, and his subordinate, being arrested. Now, she was taking over his position with a mandate to put in place new company processes that would ensure clever criminals couldn't steal from the company again. Pauline's thinking around arriving early was that she'd familiarize herself with the neighborhood before starting work. But she'd forgotten how draining the journey was. Steamships may have been slow but at least you rested and acclimatized as you traveled. You didn't get to do it all in one afternoon at the end of a solid day of admittedly upmarket business class travel. At this moment, she felt so tired, she might just spend the extra days sleeping.

Then, through the balcony door of her room, she could hear children splashing in a pool. It sounded enticing. A swim seemed the perfect way to cool and unwind. With her unpacking done, she changed into her swimsuit, threw on a robe, grabbed a pool towel, and made her way out into the sunshine.

After a dozen lazy lengths of the pool, avoiding cannon-balling boys and splashing, shrieking girls, she climbed out to lie on a lounger beneath a huge umbrella. The last thing she needed was a sunburn on her first day. As she'd hoped, the water had woken her tired mind and she ran through her options. Walk around Lithgow on the following morning to scout out a place to live, or rent a car to tour the nearby country? The driver had told her he'd be back to pick her up at eight o'clock Monday morning, so she had two whole days of the weekend to enjoy her new surroundings.

Of course, the surroundings weren't entirely new. She'd been here on assignment only three short months ago. Then it had been winter in New South Wales's Blue Mountains; there'd even been one morning with a light dusting of snow, to the delight of the local schoolchildren who were given the day off. Now it was heading into full summer, and to Pauline's unpracticed eye, it looked no different – except around the motel's property where purple-flowering trees were in bloom. For the rest, the bush covering the sides of the mountains looked the same. The gum trees still had leaves and were still shedding bark, completely contrary to her northern hemisphere ideas.

Summer in a motel full of touring visitors didn't appeal. Tomorrow, while re-acquainting herself with Lithgow, she'd look for a house to rent in a quiet neighborhood, with a garden. She wouldn't get any gardening done. Miss Marple may love gardening, but she wasn't yet sure Miss Riddell did. Still, she had to have one as a place to relax and enjoy the sunshine. With that decision made, Pauline rolled over onto her front to get some sunlight on her back. She'd only been out of the water fifteen minutes lying under the umbrella, but she could feel her skin prickling in the heat.

Next day, after an early breakfast, she began her reconnoiter of the town. It was small enough to walk around. The town was strongly reminiscent of home with areas named for the places its early inhabitants came from in years gone by, like Vale of Clywdd, Geordie Street, and the name Lithgow itself. The regions of mining and ironworking in Wales, England, and Scotland.

Throughout the town were many bungalows, one-level homes set in their own gardens, all looking exactly like what she wanted so she felt she'd have no trouble finding one that met her needs. She called into the real estate office on the main street and was given pages of properties to rent. As it was by then midday, and too hot for her, she returned to the motel to have lunch and read the sales pages by the pool.

Sipping an ice-cold water, Pauline carefully selected three houses nearby that she could walk to in the afternoon sun. And, when she was rested, she dressed and set out to look them over. Of the three, she found one that completely fitted her requirements. It was on a quiet street, had a small garden complete with elephant grass at the front that reached up to the roof, almost obscuring two beautiful stained-glass windows, and was partially furnished, empty of tenants, and ready for her to move in. She returned to the real estate office, only to find it had closed for the day. She decided to look at more homes the following day, Sunday, after church, but was confident the one she'd already picked would continue to be her favorite.

2

SETTLING INTO A NEW HOUSE

Pauline dropped her suitcases in the hall and closed the door behind her. It had been an eventful week with taking over the leadership of a suspicious and demoralized finance department and in her spare time being shown through houses for rent. Her first choice, however, had remained her first choice and, after some minor repairs, signing of papers, and handing over of keys, she was in the house on Friday evening, only a week after landing in Australia.

There hadn't been a soul on the street when she'd parked her company car in the driveway. Everything was as quiet as it had been when she'd first seen the house, been shown around, and now taken possession. It was as quiet a neighborhood as she could have wished for.

After opening the stained-glass windows, a feature she'd liked at once for their church-like character, to air the rooms and making a scratch meal from the few items she'd bought on her way over from the real estate office, she spent the evening unpacking. In the living room there was a TV, which she eyed with dislike. She couldn't believe it would be any more watchable than the little she'd seen of TV at home. There was also an old radio, which she switched on and found a music station, where a man was singing about *Old Wallerawang*, which seemed suspiciously knowing. Wallerawang was only a few miles down the road and its power station happened to be the principal customer of the company for which she was now Director of Finance. It wasn't a song she liked, she decided, much too maudlin, so she kept turning the dial until she found a station playing classical music.

Tomorrow was Saturday. She felt she could allow herself extra time in bed. She'd get up at 7:30, have breakfast, and go adventuring. First, however, she'd have an early night. The jet lag from getting to Australia seemed to have seeped into her bones and wouldn't leave. She still felt exhausted by day's end. Maybe it was also the stress.

Her sleep was broken around two in the morning by an argument somewhere nearby. Groaning, Pauline pulled a pillow over her head and tried to shut out the voices. Eventually, and it felt like a lifetime, the argument stopped. Silence once again reigned throughout the house and Pauline fell asleep.

3

THE SHOWER

PAULINE'S SLEEP lasted until the sky began to grow light. From that moment the dawn chorus of bird calls grew louder and louder until it was deafening. In England, the dawn chorus was a melodious sound from blackbirds, thrushes, and a host of warblers. This one was a raucous screeching that sounded like parrots, jays, and crows, without a songbird among them.

She stumbled out of bed and drew back the curtain. At the end of her garden, two trees were alive with birds, all screeching at the top of their voices. Pauline began to laugh at the absurdity of life. Quiet neighborhood, indeed. Quiet if she ignored the quarreling couples walking past in the night and the roosting birds' morning greeting of the sun. Shaking her head, she headed to the bathroom. A shower and then breakfast would start her day, just a little earlier than planned.

The bathroom, the agent had told her, had once been a bedroom, which explained its size. It was much larger than a usual bathroom and that made the shower, in one corner, and the basin on a wall some distance away, look strangely unconnected. The rest of the room was empty except for a tall, wooden cupboard for towels.

Pauline set the shower running and waited for it to warm as she looked around the room wondering how to make it more homely during her stay. When the temperature was to her liking, just the edge off cold, she slipped off her robe and stepped into the cubicle, pulling the opaque shower curtain closed behind her. She let the warmish water soak her hair and run down her face, washing out the last traces of sleep. Reaching for the shampoo, she was suddenly aware of someone in the room with her, just the other side of the curtain. She turned quickly to face the curtain, placing her back to the cubicle wall, but could see no shadow, no silhouette, where she expected she would. Nevertheless, she knew someone was there. Grasping the only real weapon she had, the shampoo bottle, tightly in her right hand she flung open the curtain with her left. The room was empty. She was stunned. She was sure she hadn't been mistaken.

Now, however, water was splashing all over the shower mat and floor and she pulled the curtain closed. Her heart was thumping, her limbs trembling, and her breath came in gasps. What had just happened? She stared at the curtain, almost unaware the shower was still pouring water over her and she was supposed to be washing herself. She stood transfixed, expecting a shadow to form on the shower curtain as she watched. It didn't but the feeling someone was there grew again. She opened the curtain an inch or so. No one was there.

Never taking her eyes off the gap in the curtain, Pauline washed, turned off the shower, grabbed a towel, dried quickly, and left the bathroom as fast as she could. Her legs seemed reluctant to move or even support her. She flopped in an armchair and waited for her body to recover while chiding herself for her silliness. On more than one occasion in her life she'd willingly put herself in harm's way and had never been overcome like this.

Finally, she was strong enough to rise and make breakfast. A good strong cup of tea would put everything right. And it did. After eating, she cleaned her teeth at the sink while her eyes scanned the room for interlopers, made herself presentable, and set out to explore.

Her destination was a local vantage point, Hassan's Lookout. A place she hoped would help her get her bearings in the district. It did more than that. The view from the top of the plateau looking down on the town, into the valleys, some filled with bush, some with small homesteads, and all bathed in bright sunshine and a warm breeze, washed away her fears of the morning. She was convinced that like Scrooge in *A Christmas Carol*, she'd been the victim of something she'd eaten the night before. It had all been a startling hallucination. With that comforting thought, she descended back down to the valley and found a place to have lunch.

4

MORE VOICES

The day had been merely warm by Australian standards, but hot, hot, hot by British ones. By the time she got home that evening, she longed for a shower. She entered the bathroom briskly, determined not to let this morning's nonsense repeat itself.

When the shower was at the temperature she desired, she pulled back the curtain and stepped inside facing the taps. She began to hum a brave song that slowly died as all the hairs on her body rose in fright. She twisted around quickly and flung open the curtain. As before, there was no one there. Leaving the curtain open with water splashing out onto the floor, she quickly washed and got out. The house was quiet, even though she knew the neighbors were barbecuing in the garden next door. So how had she heard the voices last night when she couldn't now hear the children chattering over the adjoining fence?

Pauline made chamomile tea and took it outside to the wicker chairs on the patio. Birds were already beginning to return to the trees at the end of her garden, which meant another early start for her in the morning. She smiled as she watched them jostling for position among the branches. Their excited twittering was a pleasant contrast to her own dark thoughts.

The fear she'd felt in the shower had nothing to do with imagination or movies, like *Psycho*, which she hadn't even seen. It was real. She had little fear of people, even when she knew they meant her harm. Her self-defense training had given her confidence and she hadn't even been scared before she'd taken the course. This was very different. And she had to spend the next six months showering in that room, for there was no bathtub.

And what of that quarreling couple last night? Were they real or had she 'imagined' that too? Tonight, she'd know the answer to that question, and it was already growing dark. Thank heavens for chamomile tea and jet lag, she thought, draining the cup. She would sleep through any lovers' quarrels tonight.

By eleven it was dark and, as she meant to make another early start on her sightseeing, she went to bed. As she'd predicted, she fell quickly asleep. A low murmuring discussion woke her just after midnight. Pauline grabbed the flashlight she'd placed at her bedside and stealthily crept out of her bedroom, peering out of the kitchen window into the garden. It was empty and nothing appeared to be moving among the shrubs, which were lit by a half-moon in a clear sky. Anyhow, the murmuring was clearly from the front of the house, and she walked quickly to the living room window.

She couldn't see anyone in the street. Frowning, she crept to the front door, opened it, and stepped outside. The neighborhood was quiet as a graveyard, she thought, and shivered. The murmuring was behind her. It was *in* the house. Unwilling to give up, Pauline walked down the path and swept the flashlight beam across the roof. She thought maybe there were animals up there. Nothing. Not a bird. Not a single thing.

She returned to the house and listened carefully. The murmuring, indistinct voices were more to the back of the house where she'd started out. She ran quickly through the hall into the main room and switched on the lights. She was alone and the voices were gone.

Pauline switched off the lights and returned to bed, switching on the bedside lamp as she slid under the cover. Tomorrow, before she went anywhere, she would thoroughly search this property and discover the meaning of this.

Her close inspection on the following morning, however, revealed nothing to explain the noises. As before, the neighborhood was quiet and the garden with its shrubs and trees had no animals hiding among the undergrowth nor burrowing under the property. A rotary clothes-drying line took up much of the small lawn and on the wooden fence that separated the garden from the neighboring house was hung a straw basket full of clothes pegs. All looked as normal as the house itself did.

The side of the house was even less likely to harbor animals or intruders. The ground was graveled and bare; the only feature of note was the heating oil tank against the wall. At the front of the house the tall cluster of elephant grass shaded, and gave privacy to, a narrow verandah looking out onto the street. A small lawn separated the steps leading to the verandah and front door from the sidewalk that ran alongside the street.

Pauline walked out to the road and looked back at the house. It still had the charm that had attracted her the moment she saw it. The white-painted wooden walls and verandah shone in the sunlight, while the two stained-glass windows either side of the door, glowed red, green, and blue. Everything about the house appealed so why was she experiencing such strange waking dreams when she was in it? She looked again at the blue corrugated-iron roof. Was this the answer? She'd never lived anywhere that had had such a thing and maybe it expanded in the sunshine and shrank during the night when it was cooling. Would that sound like people talking?

By nine she'd satisfied herself there was no natural explanation to be found at the house. She would have to widen her search if she was to get to the bottom of this minor mystery.

Meeting the neighbors sometime today, for they would be out in their garden once the children were up and fed, would be her best place to start. She'd already decided her neighbors to the north were part of the answer for they fitted the scenario that the voices were building in her mind. As she'd listened to the murmuring, she imagined a couple with a small child or children. If she handled her questions right, the answers she received would confirm the image she'd developed from the voices. Everything would soon be explained.

5

INVESTIGATING THE VOICES

When she heard the mother and children in the garden next door, Pauline took out her few small items of washed clothing to hang on the drying lines. Immediately after she exited the door, her eyes met the woman's and Pauline smiled.

"Hello," Pauline said, loud enough to be heard over the chattering children. "I'm your new neighbor."

The woman introduced herself as Penny and her children as 'noisy'. She added that she hoped their noise wasn't annoying Pauline.

Pauline said they weren't and then continued, "Unless it was them I heard arguing last night after midnight." She smiled to show she wasn't really upset.

Penny thought for a moment. "No," she said, slowly. "Last night they slept through. They run about so much in the day, they usually do sleep at night. I can't promise they won't sometimes wake at night, but it isn't often."

"Maybe the house on this side," Pauline said, pointing to the garden on her left, "had the upset last night."

Penny laughed. "Old Mrs. Creighton's children are long flown," she said.

Pauline frowned. "I was sure I heard children," she said. "I must have been dreaming."

"You're English, aren't you?" Penny asked.

Pauline confirmed this and explained her recent arrival. "I'll be here at least six months," she said, in conclusion. "I was so lucky this house was available. It's a lovely spot, so quiet and private."

"It is a nice neighborhood," Penny said. "We've only been here four years, but we know practically everybody, and they are all so helpful."

"Who lived in my house before?" Pauline asked.

"Nobody for a while," Penny said. "It seems to get rented out to people like yourself, people in town for only a short stay. I think it's a shame because it's such a pretty house. It deserves a proud and conscientious owner."

"It is pretty," Pauline said. "I loved it the moment I saw it. I wondered who had installed the stained-glass windows. They shine such wonderful colors into the front rooms."

Penny shook her head. "Long before our time, I'm afraid," she said. "Mrs. Creighton would know."

"I haven't seen her yet," Pauline said.

"She's very old now and is rarely outside, which is also a shame, I think," Penny said. "I'm going to sit in the sunshine every day when I'm old."

"I would too if I lived here," Pauline agreed. "I don't want to make a nuisance of myself asking her questions about my new home, so I'll wait until she ventures out."

"Most Sunday mornings she goes to chapel," Penny said. "You'll see her then. She walks right past both our front doors."

With her plan for further investigation established, and some disappointment that Penny and her children weren't the source of her midnight voices, Pauline finished hanging the washing on the line and returned to the house. The real estate office may also be able to help.

6

NEIGHBORS AND REAL ESTATE SAY NO VOICES

THE WOMAN at the real estate office, however, couldn't help, when Pauline called in next day on her way home from work. They'd only taken over the letting of the property a year ago. Before that, it had been in the hands of an office that was now closed. They'd bought the listings but not the history.

"And the previous renter," Pauline asked. "When he or she left, did they mention anything unusual about the house?"

"Is there something unusual?"

"Well," Pauline said, realizing this would sound nonsensical to the woman, "I hear voices at night, and I can't find a reason for them. It isn't the neighbors, and the street is quiet when I look out."

"Sounds carry farther at night," the woman said.

"Yes, I expect that's it," Pauline said. "I just thought I'd ask if previous tenants had a similar experience."

"There've only been two since we began letting it," the woman said, "and they both said they were very happy with the house."

"Then I expect it's as you say," Pauline agreed. "Voices carrying at night."

Pauline left the office feeling she'd given the woman the impression she was a neurotic, but it couldn't be helped. There would be a sensible answer to the experiences and, right now, sounds carrying farther at night was as likely as anything.

The following day at work, she called all her direct report managers into a conference room. It had been a week since she'd taken over and time for her to begin setting out their new direction. She began with what she hoped would be a softener, something to win them over to this new broom brought in to clean house.

"Gentlemen," she said, looking at their expressions for clues, "it was good to see that some of the recommendations I and my colleague made only a few months ago have already been implemented or are being implemented. I'm not going to interfere with you and your people while you finish that work." She'd learned over the years starting with praise was a good strategy.

There was a neutral silence from the five men, which suggested they were at least not completely hostile.

Pauline continued, "As that work continues, however, I want to meet with each of you and your staff and get more information from them. They provided many of the ideas we recommended, and I feel they could give more if we ask the right questions."

"When are we going to do this exactly?" a grim-faced manager of accounting asked. "We're staffed for regular work, the staff are already working on implementation of new processes, and now we're to pull them aside for brainstorming sessions as well?"

"I understand and to minimize the effect, we in this room will organize the brainstorming sessions so they fit in without too much disruption," Pauline said.

The manager of receivables sighed and stared up at the ceiling.

"Mr. Hobson," Pauline said. "Are you tired?"

The man glared back at her. "We're being put through the wringer by your report because a couple of criminals couldn't keep their hands out of the till," he said. "They might go to jail but we're in purgatory. So, to answer your question, yes, I am tired."

Pauline let an ominous silence develop before answering. When she felt they were sufficiently on edge, she said, "What happened here may have been the criminal activity of two men, that's true. But everyone in this room had a responsibility in seeing such wrongdoing and stopping it, or at least alerting the board to what was going on. None of you did that, which leaves the impression you are incompetent, or you were in on it. Either way, you are lucky to be continuing in your jobs at this company. To the first possibility, I'm having appropriate training organized for you and your section managers, and to the second, we will have processes in place to see nothing like this happens again."

"Training!" the man said. "I'm a certified professional and I've been doing this job longer than you've been out of school."

"Nevertheless," Pauline said. "You will all attend training to identify unusual patterns or activities."

"I guess it beats working," he said to the others.

"Mr. Hobson," Pauline said quietly. "Your presence in

this meeting is no longer required. You and I can take this up right after in my office."

He swept up his folders, pen, and coffee mug and stormed out of the room.

"Now, gentlemen," Pauline said. "We will continue."

Pauline returned to her office and called the head of security, asking for an officer to come to her office right away. She had her secretary type out a short letter, signed it and waited. When the security officer arrived, she called Hobson and asked him to come to her office.

He entered the room, and she was pleased to see he was calmer than he had been when he'd left the conference room.

"Mr. Hobson," Pauline said. "I've been brought here, halfway around the world, to put in place an organization that will prevent future wrongdoing and that's what I will do. You clearly have a problem with that." He began to speak but she held up her hand to silence him.

"There is no more to be said, Mr. Hobson," Pauline continued. "I must have a team that's with me. Here is the notice of termination of your contract," she held out the envelope. "Mr. Johnson here," she nodded to the security officer, "will escort you to your office, where you will remove all your personal belongings, and he will then escort you off the premises. Good day to you." She nodded dismissal and opened the file that lay on her desk. She kept pretending to read until she heard the outer office door close and then sighed with relief. It was a most unpleasant occurrence but one that would bring the others to heel and quash any further thoughts of rebellion.

7

HER NEIGHBOR REMEMBERS

Penny, her next-door neighbor, had told Pauline that Mrs. Creighton, her other more elusive neighbor, only appeared when going to chapel. The following Sunday, Pauline was dressed for church and watching from the window around the time she knew Mrs. Creighton must set off walking.

Her vigil was rewarded when she saw the old woman appear on the sidewalk outside her house. Pauline exited her own door quickly and joined the old woman as she slowly walked past Pauline's door.

"Good morning," she said brightly. "I'm your new neighbor in number forty-five. Pauline Riddell," she added, holding out her hand. There was no return handshake.

"You're a Pom," the old woman said.

Pauline laughed. "I am," she replied. "Just arrived two weeks ago."

The old woman nodded. "My Ron was a Pom," she said.

"Then we have more in common than just a garden fence," Pauline said, still smiling. Hoping to see a glimmer of life in the expressionless face.

"How do you like the house?" the old woman asked after a moment.

"I like it a lot," Pauline said. "I was wondering if you could tell me about the previous owners."

"It hasn't had an owner in twenty years or more," Mrs. Creighton said. "People are put off by the murder-suicide. It's always just rented."

"A murder and a suicide," Pauline cried. "I wasn't told that."

"Well, you rented it from those new people on the main street. They wouldn't know. They only arrived yesterday themselves."

"Can you tell me about the events?" Pauline asked.

"It was a long time ago," Mrs. Creighton said. "I may have a lot of it wrong now."

"Well, who was murdered?"

"Mrs. Langton was her name," the old woman said. "Though they never found her body. Some people think she just ran away but she didn't. She's out there somewhere," she added, pointing her stick at the looming bush-covered hills.

"And the suicide?"

"Her husband, the one who murdered her," Mrs. Creighton said.

"Was he a violent man?" Pauline asked.

The old lady shook her head. "Too soft if anything. They both were. Such a lovely couple when they moved in. Then they had a daughter. One of those that screams and shrieks if she doesn't get her way."

"Maybe the baby wasn't well," Pauline said. "When babies are teething—" She was interrupted by the old lady's harsh laugh.

"I had three children of my own, Miss Riddell. You did say 'Miss' didn't you?"

Pauline felt herself blushing light pink at the woman's evident belief a mere 'Miss' would know nothing about children.

"I wondered if there was a reason for her screaming, that's all," she said, knowing it sounded defensively lame.

"Nothing a firm spanking wouldn't have fixed," Mrs. Creighton said shortly. "But they were modern and didn't believe in such things, so the little demon tore them to pieces. Not many kids are that way but when they are, it's usually a girl."

Pauline was sure she too would be a modern parent, if circumstances allowed, and decided not to argue the point.

"You think they fought over the child?" she asked.

Mrs. Creighton laughed harshly. "Maybe, this was before your time," she said, "but did you see a film called *The Bad Seed*?"

"I think I may have done," Pauline said guardedly. She suspected she hadn't. It didn't sound the sort of movie she would have approved of.

"It was in the cinema here around the time," Mrs. Creighton said, "and it described that child exactly. They didn't so much fight *over* the child, the child simply set them at each other's throats."

"But how old was she?"

"When her mother took her to her parents, she would have been about four," Mrs. Creighton said. "But they took her away too late. Mrs. Langton said it was to let her and her husband get back to being as they were, but the trouble was already too far gone."

"But if he was as soft as you say," Pauline asked, "why didn't they recover?"

"He was a nice man, but a bit of liquor and he became passionate, as so many do," Mrs. Creighton said. "I don't mean amorous," she continued. "I mean argumentative and angry. By then, he'd taken to having more drinks than were good for him."

"His wife obviously thought he would recover," Pauline said thoughtfully.

"And he might have, but the rumors about her and another man were swirling around the town, though there was never any proof."

"Oh, dear," Pauline said, "it was a situation likely to explode, by the sound of it. But could a child of that age do so much harm to two nice adults?"

"Every once in a while, one of these children ends up in the care of people too weak to hold their own. Firmer parents would have put an end to it quickly, but they tried to appease her. You can't appease that sort. Only stand your ground and show them who is the parent and who is the child," Mrs. Creighton said. "Neither of them had it in them. If they'd been chapelgoers, they would have known such wickedness is often around us, but they weren't and thought the best."

"I'm a church-goer myself," Pauline said, "but I don't see how that helps."

Mrs. Creighton's expression showed exactly what she thought of church people. "You wouldn't understand because your bible studies are all about how lovely everything is and you never look at the whole range of human characters, good and bad, the bible gives us."

"I think we *should* look for the best in people," Pauline said.

"And that's why someone like little Eve Langton would eat you for breakfast, lunch, and dinner, as she did her own parents," the old woman said. "There is evil in the world, Miss Riddell, and it isn't all down to the way they're brought up. Sometimes it comes fully formed."

"Surely not," Pauline said, aghast at the old woman's harsh assessment of a toddler.

"Here's where we must part company, Miss Riddell," the old woman said, stopping outside the small Methodist chapel. "You, I imagine, are going on to the Unifying Church down the road."

"I am," Pauline said. She saw the old woman struggle to lift her foot onto the low step that led up to the chapel door. "Can I help you?"

The old woman swung around angrily. "Young woman, I've been climbing these stairs for longer than you've been alive. I don't need your help. I don't need anyone's help!"

Despite this rude rejection, Pauline watched the old lady climb unsteadily to the door before walking on with her mind in a turmoil. The old woman's description of the family was the picture that had formed in her mind as she'd listened to the voices. A quarreling couple and a shrieking child. She had to talk to Mrs. Creighton again. She needed to know more about the murder and the suicide. When she'd first heard the voices, she thought it was a couple passing in the street. She hadn't thought of the voices as trying to frighten her. And the presence she felt in the bathroom was frightening but, she thought, not trying to harm her. Were they a cry for help?

All through the service, Pauline pondered the one simple question underlying everything that was happening. Was she going mad or did these things exist?

8

MISS RIDDELL MUST INVESTIGATE

Returning from church, Pauline had lunch and waited until she was sure Mrs. Creighton would be home before she walked around to her house and knocked on the door. As she'd expected, it was some time before the old woman arrived at the door and slowly opened it. Her expression was as grim as it had been when Pauline had walked with her to chapel, and it didn't change when she saw Pauline standing there.

"I'm sorry to bother you, Mrs. Creighton," Pauline said, before the old woman could slam the door shut. "I would like to know more about the Langton family and what happened to them."

The old woman considered for a moment and then stepped back; Pauline entered. It was dark inside and the furnishings were also dark, and very old. Pauline followed the woman down the narrow hall to a larger sitting room with windows that faced west and welcomed the afternoon sun.

"Sit," Mrs. Creighton said. "I don't have anything in the afternoon so I can't offer you tea."

Pauline smiled. "I've just had my afternoon tea," she replied, "and I don't need anything, thank you."

"I want my nap so ask your questions and then go," Mrs. Creighton said tersely.

"What happened to them?" Pauline said. "That's all I want to know. I can look up the details if I want to get deeper into it."

The old lady frowned. "I don't know exactly," she said. "Mrs. Langton had fallen out with me by the end."

Pauline could understand that, but she said nothing.

"One day, she just wasn't there," Mrs. Creighton said. "Mrs. Langton, I mean. I'd heard them arguing the night before. You can hear everything in these houses the walls are so thin, but it was quiet the next morning."

"What did he say?"

"He said nothing until the evening. Then, he told the police his wife was there in the morning when he went to work but wasn't home when he returned. When she didn't come home early in the evening, he'd gone to places she might be. She wasn't at any of them and hadn't returned when he got home around midnight. They said they couldn't start searching right away because she was an adult and could leave her home at any time without having the police hunt her down."

"But she didn't come back?" Pauline asked.

The old woman shook her head. "Some of the men organized a search and they looked for days but they found nothing. Then, after a few days of searching, the husband, Bruce was his name, hanged himself and that seemed an end to it. You couldn't ask for a clearer admission of guilt."

"Did he hang himself in the house?" Pauline asked, puzzled. "It's only one floor. How did he do it?"

"Their bedroom had one of those swag lamps that hung

from a hook in the ceiling. Apparently, he fastened his belt around his neck, hung the loop over the ceiling hook, and kicked away the stool he was standing on."

"He must have been in awful anguish to take such a way out," Pauline said.

"I imagine guilt does that to a decent man," Mrs. Creighton said, "and in his sober moments he was a decent man."

"In their bedroom, you said," Pauline continued. "Which room would that be?"

"The one at the back of the house," Mrs. Creighton said. "It's the biggest one of the two."

"It's a bathroom now," Pauline said, her insides fluttering in excitement.

"Is it?" the old woman said. "I didn't know that."

Pauline returned to her house and walked into the bathroom. She stood at the door and imagined the room as it would have been all those years ago. Where would she put the bed? When that was settled in her mind, where would that swag lamp have hung? She could almost see the room as it was then: the bed, the clothes closet, and the lamp, placed where it could be switched off by someone once they were in bed. The swag lamp would have hung, she was sure, where the shower stall now stood.

Pauline continued for a moment in deep contemplation. She had more than enough on her plate with work and looking after herself in a new home, a new town, and a new country. She hadn't time for investigations and certainly not investigating a twenty-year old case that was as open-and-shut as this one was. A bad seed daughter Mrs. Creighton had said, a man who drank when he shouldn't, and perhaps an adulterous wife.

But Mrs. Creighton was a censorious, bitter old woman.

How easily the description could have been 'an unhappy or ill child, a man who loved his wife and child very much, and a wrongly smeared woman' if the story had been told by a more sympathetic observer. And if that view of the events was true, how likely was it the accepted story was true?

Still, the voices and, she struggled to find a better word for it, the presence she felt, seemed in many ways to corroborate the story she'd been told. And that returned her to her earlier questions. They were certainly alarming but were they threatening? She thought not. As her intuition had suggested, she felt someone asking her to investigate. As no one here in Australia knew that's what she was famous for, she might well assume the call came from beyond the grave. That, of course, was totally impossible and, also, contrary to her own beliefs. There were no ghosts of dead souls wandering the earth looking for justice or vengeance. And yet, she'd never in all her life experienced anything like this.

Having almost established to her own satisfaction it couldn't have come from dead souls, Pauline decided the cry for help could only have come from her own spirit or soul. Perhaps, even though she hadn't heard the story when the experiences began, somehow her own mind had sensed it and was demanding she do something about what had happened here so many years earlier. That wasn't a satisfactory explanation either because she didn't believe in clairvoyance, but it was better than believing in ghosts.

9

A MORE REASONABLE WITNESS

HAVING DECIDED SHE WOULD, how was she to investigate? Where should she start? What did she know? She knew the names of the couple, where they lived, and that they had a daughter who was sent to her grandparents in Bathurst. The local records office could provide much of the information she needed, including the woman's maiden name which would help find the daughter who might still be living nearby. Bathurst wasn't so very far away. One or other of the grandparents could still be alive. After all, it was only twenty years ago. She wished she'd asked Mrs. Creighton for their names. Then Pauline remembered Evan Morgan, one of the accountants in her own department, telling her how he'd lived in the town all his life. She'd start with him.

"Evan," Pauline asked at work the next day as she saw him making his way down the corridor that led past the accounting office, "have you got a minute?"

"You're the director," he said drily. "My time is your time, from nine to five."

"This isn't work-related," Pauline said. "It's about an incident that happened in Lithgow about twenty years ago. Do you remember the Langton family tragedy?"

He nodded. "Of course, I remember. It was bad. Wife and husband dead and a kiddie orphaned."

"It seems I live in their house, and I'd like to know more about the events."

"Why?" Evan asked. "It will only make you uncomfortable in the house, surely."

Not more than I already am, Pauline thought sarcastically. "I'm not superstitious," she said. "It won't bother me. My neighbor was telling me about it but she's very old and her memories have faded. I thought your memory might be sharper."

"Old Mrs. Creighton's as sharp as she ever was," Evan said, laughing. "She just doesn't take to strangers right away."

"Old people are often like that," Pauline said, smiling. "Can you tell me where I might find the daughter who was sent to Bathurst?"

"I see," Evan said, his grin growing broader. "Did Mrs. Creighton mention Jezebel when you asked?"

"She was very biblical," Pauline said, puzzled, "but she didn't directly mention Jezebel, no. Is that the girl's name?"

Evan shook his head. "No. Her name is Eve, usually called Evie by her few friends, but her behavior makes her a Jezebel or Delilah in Mrs. Creighton's mind."

"Oh, dear," Pauline said. "She hasn't turned out well, then. If Mrs. Creighton thinks she's one of those kinds of wicked women."

Evan shrugged. "She's wilder than most young 'uns today but no one cares about that sort of thing nowadays, do they. Except for the Mrs. Creightons of the world, obviously."

"Sadly, they don't," Pauline said. "That pill has ruined the lives of many young women who felt they'd been freed from nature's restraint."

"I doubt Eve would have worried much, even without the pill," Evan said. "She has an appetite for pleasure, of all kinds, that won't be restrained by man or nature."

"You make her sound quite frightening," Pauline said.

"Then I'm overdoing it," Evan said. "She's just wilder than most, that's all. You'll have no trouble finding her. Fortunately, for the Mrs. Creightons of the district, she confines herself to leading the younger crowd in town and doesn't bother the likes of us."

Pauline frowned. "Are her grandparents still alive?" she asked. "I don't think Eve will remember any of the events of the time. She was too young."

"Her grandmother is," Evan said. "She might know more about her daughter's thoughts at the time than we would. Her name was Shelagh. People joked they were made for each other because of their names, Bruce and Shelagh. The perfect Aussie couple."

"Then I shall talk to the grandmother," Pauline said. "And you, you were a young man then, did you know the Langtons?"

He nodded. "Yes," he said. "They weren't close friends, but this is a small town, and all of us knew each other to some extent."

"What can you tell me about what happened?" Pauline asked.

Evan looked both ways along the corridor before saying, "I think it would take some time and may be best discussed in private."

Puzzled, Pauline said, "If you think it best. Come to my office when work is over. It will be quiet enough then."

It was well past quitting time when Evan appeared, which intrigued Pauline. What didn't he want anyone hearing him say? Who in the offices would be upset if they knew he was talking about ancient local history?

"Some people are still sensitive about the events," Evan explained. "The police questioned lots of the men who knew Shelagh because the rumor mill had said she was having an affair. It made for a lot of unpleasantness at the time and for some time after. For some people, it is still a sore point."

"Were you questioned?"

Evan appeared to hesitate before answering. "I was and I was as angry as the others, I can tell you. I'm chapel, see. We don't do that sort of thing and being accused like that makes it awkward, both in chapel and in gatherings."

"But you're not angry now?"

"No," he said. "It was a long time ago and the sting has gone out of it."

"I'm glad," Pauline said. "I wouldn't like to think my idle curiosity was upsetting to you or anyone."

"Then I'll tell you who you shouldn't talk to," Evan said. "One man, Gerry Davies, lost his wife and family over it. She wouldn't believe the police would ask questions if there was no cause. Very strict chapel, she was. Another man, Rory Chalmers, was held for questioning in a cell for days and was shunned by his fellow congregants for years after. Presbyterian Scots are as strict as we Welsh Methodists, see?"

"Thank you," Pauline said. "I'll be certain to avoid the subject when they are around. What do you remember?"

Evan frowned. "I didn't see what was going on right away," he said. "I don't think many of us did. Shelagh was struggling with the little one – the kid was a holy terror even then."

"Mrs. Creighton said that too."

"She would," Evan said, grinning. "Then Bruce, who would barely touch a drink after work when he came out with us, began having more than one. We said he was finally loosening up, letting his hair down. And we really thought that... he was just becoming a regular mate."

"I see," Pauline said, when Evan seemed lost in the past.

"Well, as I said," he continued, "Shelagh stopped going places because the kid caused a scene wherever they went: church, shops, library, everywhere. Bruce stayed longer at work and then when we had our Friday pub night, he stayed even longer." Evan shook his head. "We should have noticed," he said, almost to himself.

"Then?"

"Then the rumors started," Evan said. "Somebody had seen Shelagh with some man. It was never clear who had seen this or who it was she was with. It was just gossip."

"It's horrible when that starts," Pauline said.

He nodded. "It is. Then it got worse. Now somebody knew the man was John, or Joe, or Jack and again, there was no one who admitted to seeing them, it was always just 'someone saw'."

"Someone was making trouble, in fact," Pauline said.

"That's what we all thought too," Evan said, "until she took the kid who was a toddler by then to her mother's place and said she and Bruce were going to sort out their lives."

"That didn't convince you she was innocent?"

"Most people said her fancy man had dumped her and she was trying to mend fences," Evan said. "You see how far it had gone by this time."

"I do," Pauline said. "No one by then believed her."

"Exactly, so when she disappeared, most people said she'd run off to Sydney leaving Bruce with the baby."

"Did you take part in the searches?"

"I did and, like most of us, thought it a waste of time," Evan said. "She was in Sydney doing what her kind always do to get by while we were being eaten alive by insects in the bush."

"Do you still think Sydney's where she was?"

Evan shook his head. "No, not now," he said, sadly. "She's out there in the bush somewhere; I'm sure of it."

"Was it her husband killing himself that changed your mind?"

'Yes and no," Evan said. "A lot of us thought she would come back when she heard he was dead. And she would have heard. It was on all the news reports and newspapers. But she didn't. That's when we knew, for sure."

"We've jumped ahead," Pauline said. "What about the searches?"

"They were thorough, even though we all had doubts," Evan said. "The police marked up the surrounding country into squares and we walked them carefully. Bruce was there. Looking as guilty as sin, everyone said."

"But was he guilty of murder or of not helping his wife when she was in such difficulty," Pauline said.

Evan nodded. "Exactly," he said. "Feelings were mixed on that question. Then, one morning, he wasn't there. There was a lot of comment, you can imagine."

"I can." Pauline nodded.

"We searched until midday, then, when we'd gathered at the rendezvous for lunch, we were told Bruce had hanged himself. That settled it for most people."

"What did you think?"

"I was puzzled and didn't know what to think," Evan said. "If he wanted punishment for killing her, why not just show us where the body was and confess? If it was because he hadn't supported her as he should, hanging himself was too extreme. Finding her in Sydney and bringing her home, or joining her there, would have been a more sensible solution."

"And if it was because she'd taken a lover?"

"He'd have taken it out on the lover," Evan said, "as any man would."

"So now you thought Shelagh must have been killed?"

"As I said, I was puzzled," Evan said. "The searches continued in the hope we would find her grave and return her to her parents for a Christian burial but that didn't happen."

"How long did the searches go on?"

"Every day for the first week and then it was cut down to evenings and weekends, whenever people had time. I went on searching for months. Quite a few of us did. In fact, even now, if I'm out in the bush, I keep my eyes open for some clue. You never know when an animal or the weather will expose buried objects."

"But that was the end of it?"

"More or less," Evan said. "Now, let me give you the address of Eve's gran and the names you'd be wise not to approach." He wrote quickly on Pauline's desk notepad and handed it to her.

She smiled. "I see why you wanted somewhere quiet to talk," she said. One of the men was in the accounting office.

Evan nodded. "Very bitter, he is. And I can't say I blame him."

"So, it never became right for him?"

"No because there was never an answer," Evan said. "Shelagh was gone who knows where and Bruce was dead. No proper answers and so no way of repairing the damage to his family."

Pauline was quiet for a moment. "Has nobody since tried to discover what really happened? Investigated more, I mean?" she asked.

"Everyone has a theory," Evan said, "even me. No one has explained it in a way that sets people like Gerry free and it's too late now."

"Have you ever heard anyone say their old house is haunted?" Pauline asked.

Evan smiled. "I never heard it was," he said, "but if a house were to be haunted here in this town, I guess it would be that one." He paused, looked puzzled, and then asked, "Is it haunted?"

Pauline shook her head. "Not really," she said. "Not spectral figures walking through walls or anything like that. I just felt something, a feeling that's all, and then when Mrs. Creighton told me the story, I was surprised at the coincidence. Anyway, thank you for filling out the story some more. I'll go and find Gran and ask for her memories, I think."

Evan said good night and began to leave the room. He stopped at the door. "Something just came to me," he said. "I did hear that Bruce killed himself after someone in one of the search parties asked him to 'show us where she's buried'."

"Do you know who?"

"No," Evan said, shaking his head. "It's like the rumors about Shelagh, 'someone said'."

10

BACKGROUND RESEARCH

When Evan had gone, Pauline dialed the number she found from the Yellow Pages and waited as the phone rang. It rang for a long time but just when she thought there was no one home, it was picked up.

"Hello?" a thin, quavering voice asked.

"Hello," Pauline said, "is this Mrs. Brown?"

"Yes," the voice replied.

"I'm Pauline Riddell," Pauline said. "You don't know me, but I now live in your daughter's old home in Lithgow, and I wondered if you'd be willing to talk to me about her time here."

There was a pause and then, "Why?"

"I love local history," Pauline said. "I'm new in town and I've found myself in a house with so much history. I realize talking about the events of that time may be painful, but I'd really like to understand what happened."

"What difference does it make now, what happened?" Mrs. Brown replied, her voice considerably stronger and beginning to sound angry.

"It might help a lot of people if it was better understood," Pauline said. "A fresh pair of eyes might just be enough to explain it."

There was another pause. "It was all so long ago," the woman continued at last. "I think it's better left in the past."

"I understand that," Pauline said, "and maybe I won't see anything new but don't you think Eve might want to know what happened to her parents?"

The old woman snorted. "Not her," she said, brusquely. "She's never given her mother a second's thought since Shelagh left her here."

"Maybe you would, though?"

Again, the pause. "Yes," she said, her voice almost a whisper. "Yes, I would."

"Then can I visit and talk?"

"If you work," Mrs. Brown said, "I expect Saturday would be best for you."

"That would be wonderful," Pauline said. "Shall we say two o'clock?"

It was agreed and Pauline hung up the phone knowing she was now committed to an investigation, and she felt the growing excitement that came with that.

Pauline rang the bell at the small house in a quiet residential section of Bathurst. She glanced at her watch to confirm she was on time. As the minutes ticked away, she continued to wait. She was beginning to feel nervous; it wouldn't be the first time she'd called at a house to discover the old woman who lived there was dead.

Then the door opened and a small woman with white hair asked, "Miss Riddell?"

"That's me," Pauline said, hoping her relief at finding Mrs. Brown alive didn't show.

Mrs. Brown stepped back, inviting Pauline to enter, which she did. The old house smelled of frangipani, a scent she'd learned to recognize on her first visit to Australia.

"Come through," Mrs. Brown said, leading the way into a pleasant, sun-filled sitting room. "I like to sit here in the afternoon," she said, "though it can get quite hot, so you'll have to tell me if you find it uncomfortable."

"I will," Pauline said, though it was already too hot for her comfort.

"Sit down," Mrs. Brown said. "I'll make us some coffee."

Pauline watched as Mrs. Brown walked with difficulty into the kitchen. She couldn't be much over seventy years old but seemed older, much older. Some illness in her life, no doubt. Or was it just worrying about her bad seed granddaughter, Eve? Whatever the cause, Mrs. Brown was stooped, and her steps faltered. Pauline didn't like to think of her carrying a hot coffee pot and decided when she heard it made, she'd volunteer to carry it through.

The problem didn't arise, however, for Mrs. Brown had one of those wheeled serving carts and pushed it into the living room quite safely.

When the coffee was poured and the plates of snacks handed around, Mrs. Brown said, "You live in my daughter's old house, you said?"

"That's right," Pauline agreed. "I'm working in Lithgow for the next six months and I took a lease on the house. It's a pretty house and so quiet."

"It was," Mrs. Brown said. "I haven't seen it in over twenty years. I couldn't bear to go, and I wanted to keep Eve away, in case it made her want her mum or dad."

Pauline nodded. She wouldn't have wanted to go back either.

"You said you were interested in local history, I think?" Mrs. Brown asked. "Why this piece in particular?"

Pauline explained as best she could the feeling she'd had in the house and then her surprise on learning something horrible had happened there. She added, "Back home in England, I like to delve into local mysteries. It's a sort of hobby," she finished lamely.

"Not being married, or a mother," Mrs. Brown said, "I suppose you would want something to spend your time on."

Pauline smiled and replied, through gritted teeth, "Something like that, yes."

Mrs. Brown continued, "Once, I would have been angry and upset at you nosing around in my personal, private tragedy but now," she paused, "now it feels like it happened to someone else."

"I'm glad the pain has eased," Pauline said, "though I'm sure it will always be there."

Mrs. Brown nodded. "Fortunately, I have two other children who have lived good, useful lives and are still with us. Poor Shelagh wasn't so lucky."

"My neighbor and one of the men at work have told me a lot about the events," Pauline said. "What do you remember of that time?"

"Shelagh had a difficult time with the birth of Eve," Mrs. Brown said, "and I thought that's where the trouble started. I realized later, it was the child that was difficult, not just the birth."

"My neighbor, who still lives next door, says the child screamed and had tantrums all the time. I find that hard to believe unless there was something wrong with her."

"There was, is, something wrong all right," Mrs. Brown said grimly, "but it isn't the sort of thing you can fix."

Pauline clearly looked puzzled because Mrs. Brown continued, "She's still a mischief maker today and she's twenty-four years old. Racing around town in the sports car her fancy man bought her, partying until all hours in the house he bought her, and high on whatever drugs or alcohol is to be found most of the rest of the time. And the man who pays for all this is old enough to be her father." She shook her head despairingly.

"It must be a worry for you," Pauline said.

Mrs. Brown laughed harshly. "A worry? She as good as killed my husband with her lunacy and has shortened my life, I'll swear. In the end, I threw her out. It was her or me was how I saw it."

"I honestly don't understand," Pauline said.

"And here's hoping you never will," Mrs. Brown said.

"So, you also think it was the baby who drove the parents apart?" Pauline asked.

Mrs. Brown nodded. "We didn't then. We felt sorry for the child. We thought it was the parents falling out that was upsetting her. Then, one day, I remember it clearly, Shelagh visited and asked if we could take Eve for a few days, just so she and Bruce could mend fences. Norman and I said we would. We loved kids, you see, and thought having a youngster in the house again would be a joy." She gave a short brittle laugh and her eyes filled with tears. "We signed Norman's death certificate with that bit of kindness."

Pauline waited while Mrs. Brown regained her composure, before asking, "And it was soon after that Shelagh disappeared, I understand."

"It was and by then we were beginning to get a sense of where the problem lay," Mrs. Brown said, "and that made us think Shelagh had skipped town having dumped the problem on us and, of course, Bruce. We were angry but, as I say, beginning to understand."

"So, you didn't think she'd been murdered?"

"Bruce Langton was a gentle soul who wouldn't have

hurt Shelagh or anyone," Mrs. Brown said. "So, no, we didn't think of murder until later."

"Did you hear rumors?" Pauline asked.

Mrs. Brown shook her head. "Bathurst is far enough away that gossip didn't travel so much in those days. Now, with all the cars and better roads, people work in Lithgow and live here so it's different."

"What did make you think it might be murder?"

"When Bruce hanged himself," the old lady said. "I thought we'd hear from Shelagh after that, but we didn't. We knew then she was dead."

"Shelagh didn't give you any indication of her problems before she turned up that day? What they were or what was happening?" Pauline asked.

"We didn't have a phone then," Mrs. Brown said, "nor did they. We saw them at weekends until sometime after the baby was born. At each visit, the child was always so disruptive they left after only a short stay. In the end, I think they were just too embarrassed to visit anymore. We didn't know anything until Shelagh left Eve with us and then, a few days later, Bruce arrived asking if Shelagh was with us. Poor man, he was desperate."

"Was that the last time you saw him?"

"Yes, he was dead a short time later."

"Did he say anything that might shed light on the events?" Pauline asked.

"He told us of the trouble they'd been having with the baby. He wouldn't even go into her bedroom that evening to see her, that's how frightened he was of her and that's when he said people were whispering about Shelagh having a lover," Mrs. Brown said.

"There was nothing else?"

Mrs. Brown shook her head. "No," she said. "Norman

went to help in the searches they organized, and the police came asking questions about a day or so after Bruce had visited. They clearly suspected him. Their questions were very pointed."

"Bruce didn't send a suicide note to you, did he?"

"He didn't, which wasn't like him at all," Mrs. Brown said. "He was a considerate man who would have wanted to explain, I'm sure."

"I imagine he was under terrible stress," Pauline said.

"That's what the police said when we pointed out his behavior was out of keeping with his character," Mrs. Brown said.

"Has anything happened since that you think shines a light on what happened?"

"Not that I recall," Mrs. Brown said. "Would you like to see a photo of them? Shelagh and Bruce, I mean?"

"I would," Pauline said. "It's odd I know so much about two people and I don't even know what they looked like."

Mrs. Brown left the room and returned with a photo album. The photos were dark and sepia-colored with age, but they showed a pleasant, happy couple enjoying picnics, swimming in a waterhole, waving from a fairground ride, a wedding, and at the last, a photo with a newborn baby.

"May I take one of these?" Pauline asked. "I promise to return it when I'm finished."

"I must have it back," Mrs. Brown said, removing one from the album.

Pauline thanked her for the photo and for talking about her daughter and what happened to the young couple and made her way to the door.

"It wouldn't be any use my talking to Eve, would it?" Pauline said as she was leaving. "She would have been too young to remember anything."

"The only time she gave any thought to her parents while she was with us was to tell *us* her own parents would have treated her better," Mrs. Brown said bitterly. "No, she will know nothing." She was about to close the door when she suddenly said, "But her fancy man might. He was one of the young people Shelagh and Bruce hung around with when they were just married."

"What's his name?"

"Fergus Drummond," Mrs. Brown replied. "He has a business on the main street in Lithgow now, insurance agent or something like that. Got money to burn, anyway."

"Thank you again," Pauline said. "I'll certainly ask him if he can shed any light on what happened." Pauline grinned and added, "I hate unsolved riddles. I think it's because of my name."

One riddle she didn't have to solve, Pauline thought as she drove away was how to get in touch with Fergus Drummond. She'd already come across that name during the investigation into wrongdoing that had brought her here. She and her fellow accountant hadn't thought Mr. Drummond was guilty of anything, but they had thought his bills were strangely higher than normal for the kind of work he'd done for the company. Of course, he could be the best at his job in the region and could charge a premium, or it could also have been the corrupt executives had padded his bills to siphon off money for themselves.

In the end, she and Keith hadn't investigated further about Mr. Drummond's bills because they had enough evidence about much larger swindles than that one – if it was a swindle. On Monday, she'd give Mr. Drummond a phone call to hear what he had to say about his invoices and that would lead to a discussion about the Langton family, she hoped.

11

MISS RIDDELL TAKES A DISLIKE

"Mr. Fergus Drummond?" Pauline asked when her secretary had linked the call through.

"That's right," a hearty male voice replied. "You're the new finance director, I understand."

"I am," Pauline said. "You seem to do quite a bit of work for us, Mr. Drummond. I'd like us to meet and get to know one another a little."

"I'd be happy to," he replied. "I was planning to get in touch with you, actually. I have several open contracts with the company, and I'd like to be sure they're still good. In case someone calls for work and I do it only to discover the new broom, if I may phrase it that way, has put a hold on them. Shall we say later this afternoon?"

"Four o'clock works for me," Pauline said. "I'll have a conference room available, so we won't be disturbed."

"That sounds ominous," he said, seriously. "Are you saying my contracts *are* on-hold?"

"I'm saying we will talk privately for this first occasion," Pauline said. "Nothing more than that."

"Okay," he said, "but we could just talk on the phone now. I could probably set your mind at ease quite quickly."

"I'm sure you could, Mr. Drummond," Pauline replied. "However, I'd like us to meet for I'm sure we'll be talking a lot in the weeks to come," she paused, "and I have another topic I'd like to ask you about, the Langton family tragedy. I understand you knew them both."

"I did," he said. "What's your interest in that old, sad tale?"

"I'll explain further when we meet," Pauline said, and wrapped up the call.

After they hung up, Pauline asked her secretary to find a small conference room that was quiet but had sufficient windows for safety. She had no reason to distrust Mr. Drummond and she wasn't planning to do him financial harm, she was just growing cautious in her maturing years.

Fergus Drummond was brought to her office a few minutes before four and Pauline's secretary introduced them. Even as he entered her office, Pauline took in the man's appearance while trying not to show her dislike.

She could see Fergus Drummond may once have been slim, handsome, and popular with women but now wealth had taken its toll. He looked the way Elvis Presley looked before he'd died last year, overweight and oily. It was as if his hair oil had crept down over his tanned, chubby face. Like Elvis, which is why she'd made the connection, his hair was as black, or possibly blacker, than it was when he was a teen. And it was still combed in that same Fifties style. It didn't look real. She mentally shook herself. Not liking someone was a warning sign; she would have to work twice as hard to maintain her objectivity as she would for someone she had no feelings about whatsoever. Still, she couldn't help hoping he'd prove to be the murderer.

"Have a seat, Mr. Drummond," Pauline said, closing the door behind them. He sat in the nearest chair and Pauline walked around the small table to the chair opposite, which suited her well for she was facing the full-length glass wall that separated the room from the corridor. She could signal for help if need be.

"Thank you for seeing me," she said. "I can imagine how busy you are at a time like this."

"Certainly am," he replied, "but when you mentioned my contract and the old Langton murder-suicide, I just had to know more. I assume you know my connection to the Langtons and that's what you want to talk about?"

Pauline nodded. "Partly so," she said, in a prim English way. "I hoped you could tell me more. I live in their old home," she added, by way of explanation. "Still, there is a sound business reason I wanted us to talk as well."

He nodded. "I heard you'd rented the old place," he said. "Is that what started you investigating?"

"Not really investigating," Pauline said. "Nothing so grand as that. The story and the fact her body was never found intrigued me." He seemed fixated on her local history investigation when he should have been concerned about her financial investigations. Did that mean something?

He laughed, though there was no mirth in the sound. "Have you dug up the garden?"

Pauline shook her head. "No. I hear it and the house were both examined after Bruce Langton was found dead."

"It was," he said, "and there was no sign of her."

"And yet she must be somewhere," Pauline said, watching him carefully for any sign of discomfort. There was none and she continued, "Now, perhaps we could talk about what I really asked you here for; your contract with us. First, I'd like to discuss your invoices and the work you do for them. I can't find any record of these contracts being put out for bids and that puzzles me."

"I can't help you there," he replied. "Your internal arrangements aren't my affair. I was asked to bid. I did and I was awarded the contract. That's all I know."

"Didn't you think it odd that no other local companies were bidding?" Pauline asked.

"I'm a land consultant," he said. "I assumed the others who were asked to bid were out-of-town and I got the contract because, being local, my costs were less."

They continued in this back-and-forth discussion for almost an hour, which gave Pauline the opportunity to gauge the slipperiness of him as a businessman and a person. She decided it was time to wind the meeting up but with one more hit on the almost more important subject of the Langton family tragedy.

"While we were talking about the present," Pauline said, "did anything awaken memories round what we set out talking about earlier? The Langton family?"

"Why would it?" He asked, puzzled. "What happened then has no bearing on the present. No, my only advice for you on that topic is to visit the local newspaper library. They could help you better than I can. I've been so busy since that time the memories have faded."

Pauline nodded. "I'm planning to visit the local newspaper offices," she said, "but I was hoping for more about them as people. The human angle if you like."

"As to that, Bruce was a good bloke, a mate," he said, "and Shelagh was the perfect wife for him. They were two peas in a pod. Quiet, shy, kind. As I say, all around good people. What happened was a real tragedy. Not like the stuff you hear on the news nowadays, where you think what happened was a fair judgment on the people concerned."

"Were you Bruce's friend or Shelagh's friend, primarily?"

"Bruce's initially. We were at school together, you know. Then he met Shelagh at work. She came from Bathurst, and then I was friends with both."

"What happened must have been a shock," Pauline said.

"A shock!" he said. "That's putting it mildly. I couldn't understand it. Maybe it's like that in every case of death or disappearance but it seemed unreal."

"You took part in the searches, I imagine."

He nodded. "I did. Then and even after, when Bruce had killed himself and we all thought the only chance of finding Shelagh's body was gone."

"So, you never doubted that Bruce had killed her and then himself?" Pauline asked.

"I didn't see any other solution," he said. "I think we all thought the same. Incredible though it was, Bruce had lost his mind, killed Shelagh, and then hanged himself."

"Did you know they were having trouble as a family before the events?"

He frowned. "I don't think I did. When they had the child, I saw less of them. Well, everyone saw less of them, but you expect that, don't you? Or at least I thought that was what was happening. Afterwards, of course, when I heard people talking, I realized I'd completely mis-read the situation. My only excuse is, being a man, we don't spend our time asking each other if we're okay. We assume if someone needs help, they'll ask for it."

Pauline nodded. "My brothers are like that too," she said. "Normally, it's fine. In this case it turned out otherwise."

"I don't think of them often," Drummond said, "but they're always there in the back of my mind."

I bet you do, Pauline thought wryly, remembering Mrs. Brown's comment about Eve Langton.

"You may have heard," he continued, "I help out their daughter Evie when she runs short. Unfortunately, and before you ask, this is a small town and my help leads to gossip, which is why I'm telling you this. I don't want you to get the wrong impression if anyone tells you about my support. She's a young woman who finds it difficult to hold down a job. I blame her guardians for that. They were too strict for a child being raised in this modern age. Nevertheless, my help is only because she is the daughter of my schoolfriend and his wife. Nothing more than that. She's young enough to be my daughter for heaven's sake. But tongues will wag."

"I'm sure the young woman appreciates the help, and your motives will be understood by most fair-minded people," Pauline said. He did seem genuinely upset that he was suspected of impropriety. She wondered if he were a chapelgoer too.

He shook his head to dispel his perturbation. "I hear the rumors," he said, "though people pretend they're whispering them when I'm within hearing. That too reminds me of Bruce and Shelagh."

"You did hear the rumors then?"

"That sort of talk goes on everywhere," he said, "and it went on then. Again, I thought it just men's crude talk. Jealous because Bruce was happily married, and they weren't. That sort of thing."

"Well, it's getting late," Pauline said, standing to signal the meeting was over. "I intend to look internally at the letting of these contracts, Mr. Drummond. I don't think it will necessarily change anything except that, when they're up for renewal, there may be a more open process."

They shook hands and Pauline walked with him to the exit. As they exchanged goodbyes, Pauline added, "If you remember anything else about the Langton tragedy, please let me know. I'm genuinely interested in those unfortunate people."

She watched and waited until he left the building, making his way out into the visitors' car park. Her senses told her this was a man who knew more than he was saying.

12

WORK IS TENSE; TOWN IS TENSE; VOICES ARE WORSE

It was late when Pauline left the office, and the parking area was empty except for her car standing alone in the executive section. It looked odd, not level. As she got closer, she realized the driver side front corner was below the rest. She knew she had a flat tire before she got to it.

Fuming silently, Pauline removed the wheel wrench from the trunk and attempted to turn the wheel nuts. They'd been put on by someone very strong or with an air-powered wrench, as she'd guessed they would be, and she was never going to be able to move them.

She returned to her office and called security, asking if they'd seen anyone near her car. They hadn't. But they could help her change the wheel. Half an hour later, she was behind the steering wheel and returning home. It was now too late to consider cooking. She arrived home, washed all the dirt from her hands, changed quickly and walked down to The Galloping Grape, the trendy new restaurant in town. It was busy but, being Tuesday and the slowest day of the week, the owner explained, they could find her a table in a few minutes. Maybe she'd like to have a drink at the bar.

After the day she'd had, Pauline felt she deserved a large sherry – or even two.

The following morning her car tires were all still up, so she drove to work and left the car at the factory's vehicle maintenance shop. An hour later, they called to say there was nothing wrong with the tire. Someone had pushed a matchstick into the valve and let out the air. They'd re-inflated the tire and returned it to the car, which they'd driven over and left in her parking spot.

For Pauline, this was chilling news. Someone here in the offices or factory had such a strong grudge against her, they were prepared to act on it. She called security and explained the situation. Their casually given promise to walk by the car on their rounds didn't give her confidence.

The question in her mind was who? Was it Hobson still having access to the property or a friend of his angry at his dismissal? Alternatively, could it be Fergus Drummond or one of his friends? Or, less likely, was it someone who didn't want her raking up the past in the Langton tragedy? Or was she making too much of a single incident of malice? Maybe, it was just someone who felt that, when the old executives were removed, they should have been promoted and not some woman flown in from halfway around the world. She would have to be more careful staying behind from now on or being alone in the parking area. That was a nuisance, but she could do a lot by working from home in the evenings and that's what she would have to do.

That afternoon, at quitting time, after another day of sullen silence on the part of most of her staff, Pauline was relieved to find her car's tires were still inflated. She drove home among the line of traffic making its way back into Lithgow along the power station road and from the various small industrial sites that bordered the road. The drive was uneventful and by the time she'd reached home, she'd talked herself into believing yesterday's incident was simply a one-off prank, unpleasant but not dangerous. She parked under the carport at the side of the house and walked around to the front door.

Even before she arrived, she could smell it. Something was dead nearby. Nearby, it turned out, was her front door where a dead, rat-sized animal, that looked like roadkill, was hanging from the doorknob. Pauline stopped. She turned and walked around the house to the kitchen door at the back. Fortunately, this door was not tampered with. She let herself in and poured a large sherry. Really, she could be an alcoholic before the six months assignment was over if she didn't win over her new staff, and maybe solve that old mystery.

As she sipped her sherry, she debated what to do. Finally, she decided it was time she interviewed the local police anyway and called them under the pretense of being frightened about the pranks. A young officer arrived around fifteen minutes later, sadly too young to answer her questions about the Langton mystery, but efficient enough to make notes of the two malicious 'pranks' that had been played on her.

As he was leaving, Pauline asked, "Are there any of the local police who would remember the Langton tragedy?"

He looked puzzled but said, "The inspector will know," he said. "He was a constable then." He stopped and grinned, "I know because he loves to reminisce about how it was his first big case. Not as a detective, you understand, just as a regular officer but still, you remember those things, I guess."

"I expect he would," Pauline said. "This is the Langton house, you know," she added, by way of explanation.

"I didn't," he said.

"How would I get in touch with Inspector..." she paused, waiting for him to fill in the blank space.

"Halleck," he said, "and you can find him at the station most days during regular hours. He's in charge there now and tied to his desk, he says."

"Thank you," Pauline said. "I'll call in tomorrow. You don't need to warn him," she said with a smile. "It is just a conversation I'm after, not re-opening the case."

Pauline left work early and drove straight to the police station, where she asked for Inspector Halleck, and after some initial reluctance, she was shown into his office.

"Good afternoon, erm, Miss Riddell?" Halleck said, as if trying to remember the name he'd only just been given over the phone. "What can I do for you?"

"Good afternoon, Inspector," Pauline said, taking the seat opposite him across the desk though noticing she hadn't been invited to sit. "I want your memories. To be precise, what you can remember of the Langton case in 1957."

"Why?" he asked, bemused.

"I've rented the house where they lived, and I've become interested in the case," Pauline said, and continued by telling him of her interest, her questions, the undercurrent of concern she felt with those she spoke to, and how, right after talking to Fergus Drummond she'd found her car with a flat tire. And this was followed immediately by the dead animal on her door.

"And you think these incidents related?"

"It's possible," Pauline said.

"I hear you've caused quite a stir in other ways too, Miss Riddell," Halleck said, grinning.

"Yes," Pauline said, "it's possible these incidents are related to events at work. I haven't ruled that out."

"But you think the old Langton case is the likely reason?"

Pauline nodded. "I do," she said. "I think the work events are very new, perhaps too new, to be responsible. But I may be wrong." She hoped he wouldn't see through her obvious ploy of using the pranks to pick his brain on an old police case.

"I would have thought it was their very newness that made them more likely," Halleck said. "Spur of the moment anger, if you like."

Pauline couldn't help wondering if all his prevaricating was just a way of not answering her question about the Langton case and replied, "Nevertheless, I would like to know more about what happened in the house I now live in. Local history is something that has always fascinated me."

"Your fascination for local history doesn't, however, warrant a busy police inspector's time," Halleck said. "Now, if you have any more evidence to give concerning the two pranks that you were the victim of, that would be an appropriate use of my time."

Now Pauline was sure something *was* odd about the Langton case. Inspector Halleck was practically admitting he didn't want to share any information about it.

"Is there something about the case that hasn't been made public, Inspector? Is that why you won't, or can't, talk about it?"

"There is nothing to tell is why I don't want to talk about it," he answered shortly. "The wife disappeared, the husband killed himself, and we never found her body. That's it."

"You never doubted the husband's suicide?"

"Nah, he was as guilty as sin. You only had to look at him to see that," Halleck said.

"Were you sure it was murder he felt guilty about?"

"What else could there have been?"

"That he hadn't supported his wife as well as he should, perhaps?"

"What are you talking about? He had a good job and kept her and the kid in everything they needed," he said. "There was no question of not supporting her."

"I meant supporting her with what was by all accounts a difficult baby," Pauline said. "Was he helping her or staying late at work instead?"

"He stayed late to make the extra money they needed now that there were three of them," Halleck said, "as any decent man would. And Bruce was a decent man, just too timid by half. But hard working and kind. No, I don't think he had anything to be guilty about there."

"If things were as you say, Inspector," Pauline said, "why might he have suddenly killed her?"

"Ah, well," Halleck said, "there was the rub. There were rumors that he must have become aware of. Suggestions the baby wasn't even his. We thought he grew to believe he was working all hours for a babe that was someone else's. He challenged her on it. She admitted it and he lashed out. Not meaning to kill her, perhaps, but when he found she was dead, he panicked and buried the body instead of coming clean."

Pauline nodded. "I see," she said. "Did you search the house and garden at the time?"

"Not right away," Halleck said, "but when it was clear she wasn't anywhere obvious, such as her parents or friends, we did. We assured Bruce it was just routine, and we weren't really suspecting him, but you could see it hit him hard. It was about a day or so later he hanged himself."

"It would be devastating to a timid, gentle, honest man, I think," Pauline said, thoughtfully.

Halleck nodded. "I thought so even then," he said. "I was a constable and part of the search. Bruce's face was gray when we started the search and white by the time we finished. I wasn't a very perceptive young man, but I could see this open admission we thought he'd killed her was too much for him."

"You never thought he'd commit suicide?"

Halleck shook his head. "Nah, he wasn't the sort. Like I said, soft. I thought he'd confess. We all did."

"Were there any sightings of Shelagh in Sydney?" Pauline asked.

"Some, but none of them *were* her. We weren't surprised. We knew she was still here somewhere."

"I believe Bruce Langton went on all the searches until he died," Pauline said. "Did anything strike you as odd during them? Did he try to steer the searches, perhaps?"

Halleck shook his head. "I don't remember being on a search with him," he said. "There were a number of separate parties, you see. He would have been with others."

"But nobody mentioned anything like that later?"

"No," Halleck said, "but then there was a restraint on speaking about him after he killed himself. I think people thought he'd done the right thing and that earned him enough respect not to be gossiped about. If you see what I mean?"

"I think I do," Pauline said. "Well. Thank you for talking about this with me. I can understand why it would be difficult for anyone to talk about."

Halleck nodded. "And we'll follow up on the people most likely to have carried out the pranks," he said. "When we've spoken to them, I think you'll have no more bother."

"How will you know who the culprit was?" Pauline asked.

"It won't matter," Halleck said. "Once they know the police are involved, they'll smarten up. You'll see."

Pauline left the police station with mixed feelings. On the one hand, she hoped Inspector Halleck was right and it was those who were upset with her at work. On the other, she still thought it might be about the murder-suicide and if they continued, she would know a lot more than she knew now. She hoped it was the latter for it meant she'd tripped over someone with a guilty conscience. She'd sure like to know what they felt guilty about.

That night, the voices were different. The adult voices were still arguing but there was no screaming child in the background. Pauline found this unsettling for it suggested her own imagination was directing the voices. They'd moved from the unhappy family, which she'd heard at the outset, to the later time when the child was gone. But this change had only happened after she'd learned the child had gone to her grandparents. The voices following what she was learning made sense, if it was just her imagination, but it still begged the question: why had she heard the voices before she'd known about the history of the house? And was the fact the house had only ever been rented since the Langton's time significant? Had others heard the voices too and moved out without saying why, being frightened that people would think them mad perhaps?

The alarm rang and Pauline slid out of bed into her slippers. Now for the shower. Her shower was as it always was. It was impossible for her to ignore the presence in the room. She'd grown used to placing towels on the floor to mop up the splashing water. She stepped inside, half closing the curtain. Her skin crawled as she washed, and she wondered how long she could keep this up. Then a thought occurred. She'd already decided the voices weren't threatening, and the presence too, while frightening, wasn't doing her any harm. Maybe it was time for her to acknowledge them both.

"I'm working as fast as I can," she said evenly. "I will tell your story before I leave, I promise."

There was no change in the room. How could there be for there was no one in the room except her, but she felt, or did she imagine, a sigh?

Quickly drying and dressing, Pauline set out for work where she anticipated another day of passive-aggressive silence from her subordinates. Sooner or later, she feared, she'd have to make an example of another of them to get the cooperation she needed.

13

MISS RIDDELL GETS SOME LOCAL HELP

AFTER LEAVING WORK, without any obvious issues with her car, Pauline went straight to the office of the local newspaper. She hadn't been able to spend time there before because she'd been working late for the first days. Now, leaving with everyone else to thwart any new pranks, she found she had an hour to spare.

She was shown into a small room, lined with shelves and binders filled with the town's history as recorded by the local newspaper.

"Is there anyone still working here who would have been here in the late Fifties?" Pauline asked as the receptionist turned to leave.

"Not anymore," the woman said. "Mr. Larsen retired a year ago. He was a junior editor then and later the boss."

"Does he live nearby?"

"Oh, yes," the woman said.

"Could you give me his address?"

"I'll phone him and ask," the receptionist said. "I wouldn't like to give it to someone without his permission."

"I understand perfectly," Pauline said. "I wouldn't want

people arriving unannounced at my house either. Tell him I'm a harmless soul looking into local history, and I live in the old Langton house."

The woman left and Pauline scanned the shelves for the right month and year. She quickly drew them out and retired to the small reading desk to peruse the story she was beginning to know so well. She'd only been reading about fifteen minutes when the receptionist returned.

"Mr. Larsen would be happy to talk to you," she said. "This evening if you're free."

"I'm free," Pauline said. "Ask him if eight o'clock would be convenient. I'd like to go home and change first."

The receptionist hurried away, returning in a few minutes with the address and confirmation Mr. Larsen would be pleased to welcome Miss Riddell to his home at eight o'clock.

After making a mountain of notes, Pauline closed the binders and returned them to the shelves. If she was quick, she could eat and freshen up before meeting someone she hoped could give her an unbiased overview of the sad events she'd set out to decipher.

"Come in, Miss Riddell," Larsen said when he opened the door. Pauline entered a neat, tidy, and masculine-decorated hallway, without any of the knick-knacks that would have been there had there been a woman in the house.

Larsen was white-haired, in his late sixties or early seventies but still an upright, vigorous man. A life of writing and office work hadn't marked him with a stoop or round shoulders as she'd expected.

"Can I offer you tea? Or something stronger?" he asked.

"Tea would be nice," Pauline said. While he was making the tea in the nearby kitchen, she studied the bookshelves that lined the walls. Once again, the room spoke of a man's sensibilities. She smiled at that thought. The pictures on the walls were ships and landscapes, rather than flowers or people.

"I understand you're interested in the Langton case," Larsen said, returning with a tray filled with cups, milk, and sugar.

"I live in their house," Pauline explained. "Mrs. Creighton, my neighbor, told me of the events and I'm intrigued to know more."

"You looked in our archives," he said. "Did that help?"

"It did, though it still leaves me wondering what really happened," Pauline said. "The story just stops without a proper ending."

"That's the fate of many stories, in my experience," Larsen said, "and even when there is an ending, I suspect it's often not the true one."

Pauline laughed. "I'm pleased to see we're already somewhat alike," she said. "I distrust neat endings to stories."

"If you've read the articles," Larsen said, "I'm not sure I can add anything more."

"I was hoping a newsman covering events at the time would have a wider view of what happened," Pauline said. "Articles are often focused on specific events. And the people I've talked to so far have only been able to show me what they were involved in and what they'd heard talked about. I hoped you could give a wider view."

"I'll try," he said, "but it was a long time ago. A lot has happened since to drown out the memories."

"A question that puzzles me is why the story just died," Pauline said. "I would have thought the local paper would have wanted to keep it going, if only for the sake of sales."

"Oh, there were always more immediate stories to boost sales," Larsen said. "This was a mining and armaments town and there were always labor troubles arising that caught the townsfolk's interest. We did offer a reward for information, and we kept it open for a year, but no one came forward. No one credible, anyway."

"I spoke to Inspector Halleck," Pauline said. "The police also looked widely for information from surrounding police districts and from Sydney. Also, without success."

Larsen nodded. "The police did put a good effort into it," he said. "Apart from the obvious fact a nice young woman was missing in their town, I think having something as newsworthy as this made them want to show what they could do. It was good for us on the Mercury, too. Sydney press offices bought our articles and commissioned their own from us. The paper was never hugely profitable so, horrific though the events were, we made the most of it."

"Hence the promise of a reward that went on for a year after?"

"Exactly," Larsen said. "We hoped, dreamed, we'd get the evidence that cracked the case. Our ticket to the big time, maybe."

Pauline laughed. "I had a friend back home who was a local reporter, and she was always hoping for the story that would carry her all the way to the big papers in London."

"It didn't happen for her?"

"It did," Pauline said, and paused. She didn't want to explain Poppy had ridden to London on stories of Pauline's successful investigations. It would sound like boasting, and that was sinful, and it would lose her the element of surprise. People would be on their guard if they knew she was a famous amateur sleuth in England. "Unfortunately, her time there led her into drink and drugs. She lost her job, became homeless, and then died, or so I heard. There was no funeral."

"You're telling me I should consider myself lucky a move to the big city didn't happen to me?" Larsen said, smiling.

"Not at all," Pauline said quietly. "Your comment just reminded me of a sadness I'd almost forgotten."

"I'll tell you the theory I was working on," Larsen said, "which I've thought once or twice since I retired, I should look into again."

"Please do," Pauline replied. "Most people are sure Bruce Langton killed his wife, perhaps not meaning to, and then took his own life. If you had a different idea, it would suggest to me my own thoughts aren't so wide off the mark."

"I wondered if Bruce hadn't been killed by vigilantes," Larsen said.

"Were feelings running so high?"

"Oh, yes," Larsen said. "Everyone was certain he'd killed her, you see, and I heard, and was told, of threats against him in conversations. It was like living in a western at times, there was so much talk about lynching."

His mention of westerns would have made Pauline smile if the subject hadn't been so serious. For her own first view of Lithgow's main street, with its raised sidewalks, had looked to her just like a town in a movie western.

"You never followed it up?" Pauline asked.

"I kept my eyes and ears open for a long time after," Larsen said, "hoping someone would let something slip. It didn't happen. And now it's too long ago. Most of the people I remember uttering the threats are dead or have moved on."

"I have a lot of experience in researching local history," Pauline said, "and I have six months of spare time to spend on it. I hope to provide a better answer, particularly for Mrs. Brown, Shelagh's mother."

"I'd forgotten about her," Larsen said. "I think you're

right. It's time she knew what happened to her daughter and Mrs. Langton deserves to know what happened to her son. She's lived with the belief he was a murderer and a suicide all these years and maybe he wasn't."

"Does she live here still?" Pauline asked, surprised no one had mentioned her.

"No, she and her husband moved to Katoomba soon after what happened and she still lives there," Larsen said, "or did until quite recently."

"Then I shall certainly interview her," Pauline said. "If she'll speak to me."

"She might be more willing if I was with you," Larsen said. "She's known me all my life, though we haven't been in touch lately, and I'd like to help with your research. You've made me feel a bit guilty about not doing it after my retirement when I promised myself I would."

"I'd be happy to have some local support," Pauline replied. "Up to now, everyone has made it plain I was treading where no treading was wanted."

"Then I suggest I make some phone calls," Larsen said, "and see if we can't get people to be more forthcoming."

"And I'll hold myself ready to interview our witnesses when you've persuaded them," Pauline said. "I also plan to make myself more familiar with the town as it was, and the places the Langtons would have known. Put myself in their shoes, so to speak."

That night, as Pauline prepared for bed, the voices were muted, distant, still there but somehow farther off. Pauline hoped it was because they, or her mind, knew she was actively answering their cry for help. Hopefully this was not just a lull before raising the drama again. Once she was started on a trail, she didn't need further pushing.

The morning shower too seemed less frightening. She

still couldn't close the shower curtain and every hair on her body still stood upright, only it all seemed less close somehow. It was possible she was just getting used to it, of course. Talking to the presence helped before, so she tried again.

"I've a helper now," she said. "You may remember him. Steve Larsen, the local news reporter at the time. He thinks there was something wrong with what happened, too."

There was no sigh this time, only a noticeable lightening of the oppressive presence around her.

Pauline stepped out of the shower, toweling herself dry. Despite being Australia in summertime, the room was cold. It always felt cold.

"Between us," she continued, "I think we will find Shelagh. It is what you want, isn't it?" *It's what I want anyhow*, she thought, while acknowledging the result may well be what everyone thought – Bruce Langton killed his wife, Shelagh, and hanged himself out of guilt.

She parked her car in her space at work and began to wind up the driver's side window, which she'd had down during her journey. The car's air vents didn't make any improvement on the cabin temperature once the sun was up and shining directly through the glass. She stopped winding with the window an inch open and, leaning across the gear shift, wound down the opposite window. Maybe having them both open would get some air blowing through the car and lower the temperature for her return at the end of the day.

As she filled her cup at the water cooler before starting work, Pauline noticed a middle-aged woman watching her from across the open office. The moment their eyes met, however, the woman looked away. Pauline tried to remember if she was one of her staff and decided she wasn't. She was obviously from a different department visiting someone here. She shook her head in amused disbelief. What was she doing? Someone visits the department, sees the department head at the water cooler and stares for a moment, and the department head imagines the woman wishes her ill. Ridiculous.

Back in her office, however, Pauline couldn't shake off the image. She wasn't imagining things. That woman really didn't like her. In that brief glimpse, that much had been obvious. She needed to know who she was. Pauline went back out into the outer office and round to where the woman had been standing.

She wasn't there now so Pauline asked the man in the cubicle, "Who was the woman who was here a few minutes ago?" Trying to make the question less accusatory, she added. "She seemed to know me, but I couldn't place her. I've met so many people these past days, it's hard for me to keep all the names and faces straight."

The man looked uneasy and unwilling to answer. After a moment, realizing he couldn't pretend he didn't know, he said, "Anthea Hobson. She's in purchasing."

"Oh," Pauline said. "Is she Hobson's wife?"

"Sister," the man said.

"I see. Thank you. I shall have to remember that. I'm sure she can't have good feelings toward me."

"I don't know if they are that close," the man said, "but firing people in a town as small as this will always turn up loyalties that weren't necessarily obvious before."

Pauline looked at him steadily. Was he warning her? Was he threatening her? After a moment, she decided he was just stating the obvious. She thanked him for his advice and returned to her office. His words gave her more to think about than just her job. In a small town, people had close ties that went back decades, and those ties were often very deep.

She still had part of her mind on this idea when, at the end of the workday, she left the office and headed for her car. It seemed to be in one piece as she approached, not in the down-in-one-corner position as before. Maybe having security walk by occasionally had dissuaded the prankster. She unlocked the door, and her nose was assailed by a pungent, disgusting smell. The driver's seat and floor were covered in a greenish goo that had clearly been funneled in through the open window. Pauline returned to her office and called the maintenance department to see what they could do to make the car drivable.

After an hour of mopping and sponging, the car was returned, though not as good as new.

"We lease these cars," the foreman said to her, somewhat accusingly, Pauline thought. "They'll want compensation if this gets any worse."

"Is there somewhere I can park the car that isn't accessible to everyone?" Pauline asked. "Inside the maintenance shop, for example."

"Not inside," he said, "but we do have a compound where we keep vehicles waiting for repairs or servicing. I'll show you."

With that change agreed for the future, Pauline drove home seething with frustrated anger. She was sure she knew who was responsible, but she'd never be able to catch her now the car was going to be safely fenced off in future.

14

TENSIONS IN TOWN AND FACTORY

That evening, she drove around to Steve Larsen's house to see if he'd made any progress. He had made very little, he said, but offered her tea and a chance to discuss.

When the tea was drunk and he'd told her who he'd called and their replies, Steve said, "You wanted to know more about the things the Langton family were familiar with or would have been a part of. We have some hours of daylight left, why don't I give you a tour?"

"All right. I'll drive, you guide," Pauline said, as they left the house, and she led the way to her car. "I should warn you, the car smells of cleaner and disinfectant." She added. "There was an incident at work today. It was the second unpleasant incident aimed at me, to be precise."

"There's a lot of ill feeling at the moment," Steve said. "You've come at a bad time. Union contracts are up for renewal and folks are goading each other into the usual 'good guys vs bad guys' battle. As someone in management, and an interloper as well, you're sure to be a focus."

"Oh, great," Pauline said, starting the engine and putting it into gear. "I thought it was just about me setting new procedures in place. I'm relieved it's bigger than that. It makes me feel so much safer."

Steve laughed. "That's the spirit," he said. "And don't forget we're about to scratch open an ugly scar from the past. You may become Public Enemy Number One."

"You're a little ray of sunshine, Steve," Pauline said. "Shining a light on my troubles and melting them all away."

"You jest but I hope that may be true," he said. "I still have some influence in this town. Turn here and we'll drive down the main street."

Pauline followed his direction, and they slowly entered the central business district of town. It wasn't large and was mainly shops.

"Here's the library," Steve said. "It's been here forever so you can be sure they knew and used that."

Pauline nodded. She'd already joined the town library and felt she knew it well enough not to ask questions.

"Along here is the cinema and farther along is the Royal Australian Legion Hall," Steve said. "I mention them together because they both show movies and the projectionist, who happens to be a friend of mine, works at both. Sometimes, there's a delay while he finishes in one place and gets the reel ready for the other. It's something of a town joke."

"I rarely go to see films," Pauline said, "but now you've told me that, I just might. It sounds like it would make even the dullest film interesting."

Her eyes were caught by the odd coincidence of the notice boards outside the places. Whether it was films that were playing, had played, or were about to play, she wasn't sure. They'd driven past too quickly to read carefully but one was *Looking for Mr. Goodbar* and the other was *The Exorcist*. It was as if the town itself was pointing out clues to her.

Had Shelagh been looking for her Mr. Goodbar and been killed when she found him? And did Pauline's house need an exorcist? Some days it certainly felt like it.

"Here we have one of our two supermarkets," Steve said. "We've become quite the modern metropolis these past few years."

"Both after the time I'm interested in, I'd guess," Pauline said.

"More or less," Steve replied. "That's the Rotunda," he continued, "and our War Memorial. A popular place to meet. Turn just along here and we'll drive down Railway Parade unless you've already been there?"

Pauline shook her head. "No," she said, "I was driven to Lithgow from the airport and haven't properly explored yet. That's what I was going to do while you sorted out people we could talk to."

They drove along Railway Parade, which was bustling with people, so a train had obviously just disgorged its passengers. It looked like the street had once been the classier street in town, when the railway was the way to travel.

"In fact," Pauline said, "other than the factory and offices, I've only been to the library, the supermarket, and the Unifying Church so your guided tour has been helpful."

"This is your first time here?" Steve asked.

"I was here for three weeks about three months ago," Pauline said, as they drove back along Main Street. "On that occasion, I hardly left the offices or my motel room at all. We generally had food delivered while we worked, it was that intense."

"You should also know," Steve said, breaking into her explanation, "Bruce Langton was in the army reserve, so they spent many evenings in the Legion. It's a lot cheaper than regular pubs and eating places."

"Perfect for a young couple with a child just starting out," Pauline said.

"Exactly," Steve replied. "Now if we turn down here, we have the small arms factory where Bruce worked."

"I thought he worked at the Hermitage mine?" Pauline said.

"He did and then got a better job, a step up in pay, at the arms factory."

"I started work in an arms factory back in England," Pauline said. "They were busy places even in the late Fifties."

"There never seems to be a shortage of wars," Steve said, "but this factory is slowly dying."

"The mine isn't so far away," Pauline said, "I pass it going to work. But the arms factory would have been closer to home for Bruce so I'm sure that would have been part of the attraction."

Steve nodded. "I imagine they thought it was going to be great," he said. "More money, a cleaner place to work, and less travel before and after. I don't know why it didn't make things better."

"Changing the subject, a little," Pauline said. "Have you heard anything about the house they used to live in?"

Steve looked at her, perplexed. "What sort of thing?"

"I don't know," Pauline said. "That the ghost of Bruce Langton haunts the place, something silly like that."

Steve laughed. "No, I hadn't heard that. Why? Does he?"

"Of course not. I was using that as an example," Pauline said. "Has anything been found there? Anything at all, really."

"Nothing," Steve said. "Why? Are you considering digging up the garden?"

"I'm tempted but I'm told that was done."

"It was," Steve said. "Before and after Bruce died. People say it was the police digging around the house that drove Bruce to kill himself and maybe it was. They really took the house and garden apart after he died, as you can imagine."

"So, I needn't waste time looking under the floors or behind walls," Pauline said, lightheartedly.

"Take the next right," Steve said, "and we'll be home. I think if there was anything in that house from those times it will be long gone. Even the couple's ghosts will have moved on by this time."

Why hadn't anyone mentioned experiencing what she was experiencing, Pauline wondered, as she parked the car outside Steve's house. It all must be in her head, there was no other explanation.

"When might you have someone set up for us to talk to?" Pauline asked.

"Come by tomorrow night," Steve replied, getting out of the car. "I have a couple of people considering it and by then I should have them convinced. I hope Mrs. Langton will be one of them."

Pauline returned to her house. Evening was drawing in and it made the house seem even more brooding. The shrubs and elephant grass sheltered it from the road, as if it were hiding, trying to be private with its thoughts. She parked the car and slammed its door; the noise made her feel more confident somehow. "What rot we do think when darkness descends," she said softly to herself as she opened the front door and stepped inside.

15

DETECTIVE HIRED FOR WORK

Pauline arrived at work, grateful her car hadn't been molested overnight and nor had her house, so far as she could see.

She walked through the near empty outer office to her own, set at the back. She was pleased to see Hobson's sister wasn't here today. She unlocked her office door, opened it, and stepped back at once. The same disgusting smell that had been poured into her car had been poured into her office. She quickly closed the door and locked it. Borrowing a phone from a nearby desk, she called security and maintenance.

While they worked to establish order and sanity back into her office, Pauline went to find the managing director. It was time that he was brought into this. These pranks were unpleasant but there was a chance they might become dangerous if they weren't dealt with.

She caught him as he was arriving, followed him into his office, to prevent him claiming a prior engagement, and explained what was happening.

"I heard about the car," he said, offering her a seat. "The trouble seems to have grown."

"It has," Pauline said. "We need a detective to investigate."

"I'm not sure the police will take these pranks so seriously."

"I mean *we* hire a detective from Sydney. He can start work in my department. Now I've stepped up Patrick Connor as Hobson's replacement, we're a man short."

"Hmm," the managing director said, thoughtfully, "how can we do that without anyone knowing? Placing the call through our switchboard would alert the whole plant, that's how gossipy the operators are, and then, when we place a contract, the purchasing department will be equally as leaky."

"I'll hire one as a private citizen," Pauline said, "provided we agree together. I can expense it and bring him into the offices."

He nodded. "Type up a contract between us," he said. "That way you'll be comfortable with the wording. We'll both sign it, and you can get the process started. Meanwhile," her boss continued, "we need to alert the police. Our insurance company will insist on it. If this does get worse and we have done nothing, they'll consider us as being partly responsible."

"I've already told the police, where my house was concerned," Pauline said, "and I now have a chief suspect for them." She explained about Hobson's sister and the long, cold staring incident.

"It isn't really proof," her boss said. "But they need to come here so it's known we're taking this seriously."

"I agree, my observation isn't proof," Pauline said. "But it is a place for them to start."

The police, when they arrived, seemed to think it was more than a starting point and interviewed Anthea Hobson for some time and then all her co-workers about her movements, which made Pauline wish she hadn't said anything. If Anthea had been angry before, she'd be incandescent with rage by the time this was all over. The worst of it was, Pauline now felt her suggestion had been based on her own anger and a need to lash out. There was no evidence. She could only hope the police found some.

Later that morning the police returned to interview her again and it was Pauline's turn to be upset.

"Miss Riddell," the sergeant began, "your accusation against this woman appears to have no foundation in truth."

"I never said I had proof," Pauline responded sharply. "I simply told you what I'd seen and why it might be suspicious."

"I think you suggested a bit more than that," he replied. "I certainly felt you were leading us to a solid suspect."

Pauline steadied her mind. "If I overdid the things I shared, I apologize," she said, as calmly as she could. "However, what I said was no more than I'd seen and knew. I take it from this you have evidence Miss Hobson was not the person responsible for these unpleasant pranks?"

"Correct," he said. "She has solid alibis for the times when these events happened."

"I'm glad to hear it," Pauline said. "Though it leaves me still not knowing who is behind them and concerned they will escalate beyond damage to property."

"I think you owe Miss Hobson an explanation as well," the sergeant said. "She's quite distraught over today's events."

"You will be continuing your enquiries, I hope?" Pauline asked.

"We will," he said, rising to his feet. "Now we've cleared the misinformation out of the way." He left with a curt nod that signaled his continued displeasure with Pauline.

She took stock of her situation for a few minutes. She was as upset as he was and not sure who she blamed most for the mess: herself for being too vehement in her statements or him for going overboard with it. Between the two of them, they'd caused an innocent woman a morning of pain and humiliation. Once again, as too often happened, she found she'd shared too much, too soon. She still hadn't learned not to do that.

Pauline sighed and set out in search of Anthea Hobson. She needed to put her part in it right as soon as possible and as publicly as possible, certainly before everyone went home and spread the story throughout the community. The poor woman shouldn't have public gossip added to her hurt.

She found Miss Hobson surrounded by well-wishers trying to re-assure her that nobody believed she could be capable of such wickedness. Pauline wanted to leave before anyone saw her but realized this was the best moment, one where there were plenty of witnesses who would relay the message far and wide.

Miss Hobson received the explanation of Pauline's part in her distress with surprising calm, unlike many of her supporters who glared and grumbled at Pauline in disgust.

"Thank you for coming to explain, Miss Riddell," Miss Hobson said. "It was kind of you. I think I understand better now this was not intended."

"Investigations are horrible things," Pauline said, "even when they prove you innocent, as the police have in this case. For my part, I'm sorry to have been the cause of your pain, it wasn't maliciously intended." Even as she said this, her doubts around her behavior remained. It was often hard to really 'know thyself', as the expression went.

After some minutes longer, answering questions from Miss Hobson's supporters, questions that grew less accusatory as the answers were given, Pauline thought it was safe to leave. Miss Hobson was smiling, her supporters too, and soon the events would be relayed far and wide. It would be no more than an exciting incident in a humdrum workday and, even better, one with a happy ending.

Pauline returned to her office to write the letter her boss had requested. By mid-afternoon, she had a short memo that she felt would stand up to any legal challenge if this went wrong. She took it to his office, they both signed it, and she left the factory to call the investigation agencies, she'd found in the Yellow Pages, from a phone box on the main street. That evening, as arranged, she once again called the agency she'd selected, and between them they finalized the details. A detective would be at her house in the morning, with a contract for her to sign. With that done, he'd start immediately.

The detective, a neatly turned out, middle-aged man who looked much more presentable than Pauline had feared, arrived at her door early the next morning. Pauline read the contract and signed it.

"You have a car?" she asked.

He shook his head. "I came up on the early train," he said. "I came straight here. I wasn't sure if you'd want me to go in today, in which case I'll find a hotel later. Or start tomorrow, in which case I'll spend the day checking out the town and do some digging about the people who work at the factory."

"Find a hotel," Pauline said, "and take a taxi out to the

plant for lunch time. We'll talk in my office, and I'll introduce you to the department after that."

He was punctual and Pauline had him shown up to her office before one o'clock, after letting it be known a new employee was arriving to help.

"What do I call you?" Pauline asked. "Do you use your regular name or a pseudonym?"

He smiled. "I'm happy with my own name, John Ventnor," he said. "That way I don't get caught out forgetting who I am."

"The agency said you'd worked on financial cases before so you can fit in here," Pauline said. "You'll need to know the background, even if you don't know our systems. I'll say you're from an agency." She smiled. "That way, as with your name, we won't have trouble remembering what we told people."

"It will be fine," he said. "Now tell me more about the staff and the incidents."

After she'd outlined recent events, and he'd made copious notes, she walked him around the department, introducing him and putting faces to the names he'd just been given. She showed him to his office, the one Patrick Connor had vacated when he'd moved into Hobson's office and left him to find his feet. With that done, she met with the managing director and let him know the detective was on site.

"I hope he can do this quickly," her boss said, grimly. "We're entering union contract negotiation times very soon and that brings its own set of problems. We don't want any suggestion we brought this fellow here to spy on union members."

"If we haven't found anything by the end of the week,

we'll stop it," Pauline said. "I think he'll get a result very soon. This prankster is too hotheaded to stop now."

"And you?" her boss asked. "How are you settling in? Are your troops carrying out your orders?"

Pauline nodded. "They are," she said, "but it takes time for new ideas to be implemented successfully so you're sure to hear some complaints." She thought it best not to explain the silent resistance she faced whenever she called a meeting or talked to the staff.

"If there are problems, you'll let me know, won't you?" he asked.

His question was somewhat anxiously expressed, Pauline thought. She wondered if there was more going on here than was obvious to her.

"Of course," she said. "I have a question though. Who initiated the contract with Fergus Drummond? I can't find a proper trail of tendering, bidding, or letting the contract and it is larger than I'd expect for that kind of consulting work."

"This wasn't in your earlier report?" her boss asked suspiciously.

"It wasn't because it had no bearing on the investigation we were doing," Pauline said. "Now I'm delving deeper into the business, I'm seeing other expenditures that don't seem to have been properly handled. I wondered if this one was approved at a high enough level that the usual processes weren't followed."

"It wasn't initiated by me or the board," her boss said, "though I did sign it on behalf of the company, as I do all major contracts. I'm sure it was explained to me at the time because I wouldn't have approved it otherwise. Are there others?"

"There are small irregularities that I suspect were initiated by various managers within their approval limits,"

Pauline replied. "This one, however, needed your signature and it doesn't have the paperwork that should have been in place. It may be a case of misfiling or even the records being inadvertently destroyed. I just thought I'd ask while we were talking off the record."

"Have it properly reviewed by one of your senior accountants and brief me on your findings by the end of the week," her boss said. "If this is another illegal legacy item, we need to put an end to it right away."

"I'll do that," Pauline said. She left his office more disturbed than she'd been since she arrived here. The MD admitted signing the contract, yet he seemed unable to explain his rationale for doing so. He didn't appear to feel guilty about it so maybe he was genuinely misled by a man he trusted. Or maybe he was just a good actor who was in on it, and it was she who needed to tread carefully over the next week as she gathered the evidence. An uncomfortable knot developed in her stomach as she considered if, in some way, she could be implicated in this wrongdoing. Was she now at risk from above as well as from below?

Pondering these questions, she sat at her desk deciding the best way to progress the research her boss had asked for. Her ponderings left her knowing she had to do it herself. She couldn't be sure anyone in her department would provide honest answers.

16

LEARNING MORE ABOUT THE PAST

THAT EVENING, her doorbell rang and Pauline, after checking through the frosted glass pane, opened the door.

"Hello, Steve," she said. "What brings you here?"

"I have found a good witness for you," he replied. "The man who was the policeman in charge of the search."

"Can we go tonight?" Pauline asked.

Steve shook his head. "He moved away years ago to Orange, which is some way past Bathurst. He's in an old people's home now. I spoke to them, and he's agreed to see us. They say he's deaf but still has his wits about him. If you leave work early tomorrow, we can go then, if you like."

The following afternoon, Steve and Pauline pulled into the pleasantly kept grounds of an older home that had additional wings newly added onto it.

"A nice place to spend your final days," Steve said, looking around.

Pauline shivered, though it wasn't cold. "It's nice," she said unenthusiastically. On balance, she thought it would be better to be murdered at seventy while trying to solve her last case than end her days in a care home, however nicely kept.

They were shown into a brightly decorated room with a view of the gardens where, after a few minutes their witness was brought in. Introductions were made by the nurse who offered them tea or coffee, which they declined.

After explaining their business and breaking the ice, Pauline said, "I'm told you organized the search for Shelagh Langton, Mr. Fortescue."

"What's that?" he asked, puzzled.

Remembering his hearing was gone and cursing the staff for not making him wear a hearing aid, Pauline said, more loudly than she liked, "I'm told you were the Police Chief in Lithgow when Shelagh Langton disappeared, and her husband killed himself. I'm looking into that tragedy."

He looked astonished. "Why?" he asked.

He clearly hadn't heard any of the explanations she and Steve had given at the outset, and she was just about to provide further background to her question when the nurse, still standing at Fortescue's side, did it for her.

When the nurse finished explaining, he nodded. "I was in the police then," he said, loudly as so many deaf people do. "We had quite a time of it, searching the bush all around town."

"How long did the search go on?" Pauline asked.

He frowned as he tried to recall the events. "About a week with everyone," he said at last. "Then maybe two weeks with smaller groups after. It was no use. If she'd been alive, we'd have found her, we almost always do in these missing persons cases, but ..." He let the sentence end; his thought unfinished.

"I understand no one has stumbled across her remains since," Pauline said.

He nodded. "That's right. Too well hidden, she is."

"I understand also her husband Bruce took part in the searches," Pauline said.

"He did," Fortescue said, "but no one was fooled. Everyone knew the trouble they'd been having. In the end, it came to one of the searchers saying 'Come on, Bruce. Just tell us where she's buried, and we can all go home.' He hanged himself that night."

"You were all that sure?"

"As a policeman," Fortescue said, "I did my best to keep an open mind but, yes, everyone knew. No one was surprised he did what he did. Kill himself, I mean. He'd looked as miserable as sin the whole time of the search. Not anxious or worried, you understand, but miserable, guilty looking."

Pauline nodded. "I see," she said. "I've stumbled into as sad a tale as any I've heard, I think."

"You have indeed," Fortescue said. "It's how we all felt, even then. Not angry or vengeful, just desperately sad. They'd been such a happy couple and there seemed no reason for what had gone wrong, but something had. You know, even on the searches, people avoided Bruce. They were both sorry and sad for him. So much so they couldn't speak to him properly. I imagine he found that hard to take."

"I imagine he did," Pauline said, seeing in her mind the scene. The lonely man walking with, and among, the others, but not one of them, shunned like a leper.

"We thought he might break down and tell us where she was, but he never did," Fortescue said, "and without that, searching was hopeless."

"Who was it that asked him to say where the body was?" Pauline asked.

The old man shook his head. "I don't remember," he

said. "It was at the end of a long day, we were hot, tired, dead beat. A group of us were sitting at our utes waiting for others so we could call it a day. It was a long time ago."

"Has nobody commented on it since? Whoever said it must have it on their conscience, I would have thought."

"I never heard of it, if they did. I'd guess they were pleased at the outcome, rather than shocked," Fortescue said. "Rough justice, I know, but feelings were running pretty high at the time. Everybody who knew Shelagh liked her. She was a nice lady."

"Was there anything about that time you couldn't account for? Couldn't explain?" Pauline asked.

He nodded. "There were lots of things," he said, frowning as he tried to remember.

"Such as?" Steve asked, when the silence seemed never ending.

"If Bruce killed her and wanted us to believe she'd run away, why didn't he take any of her clothes away with the body?" Fortescue said. "If your story is your wife has run away, you'd do that to make it look plausible, wouldn't you?"

Pauline nodded. Her excitement building. Here was something new. "Is that what he said? That she'd run away?"

"Not as such," Fortescue said. "Rather, we presumed that from his insistence we look wider."

Pauline frowned. "Were there other things?" she asked.

He nodded. "Why didn't he leave a note?" Fortescue said. "He was the sort of man who'd explain to death even the smallest deviation from normal and yet, no note. It wasn't right."

"But you do think he killed her?" Steve asked.

"Oh, yes," Fortescue said. "Unlikely though it seemed, I believed he did. What puzzled me was, had someone killed him?"

"Was there evidence to suggest someone had?" Pauline asked eagerly. She felt she was really beginning to hear more than they'd learned from anyone else.

His expression became grave, and he shook his head. "No," he said. "Our forensic people looked carefully, I made sure of that but there was nothing."

"Maybe knowing everyone believed he'd killed his wife and the fatigue of searching each day just made him act impulsively," Pauline said.

He nodded. "That's what I decided in the end," he said sadly. "Months after, when Shelagh still hadn't turned up, and there were no other suspects, I decided I must have got it all wrong and those small anomalies meant nothing."

They thanked him and left him alone with his memories. Pauline, her expression a mixture of excitement and puzzlement, said to Steve as they exited the building, "We now know the police were unhappy with the case, which is something I didn't know before."

"It doesn't help us though," Steve said. "It leaves us exactly where we were."

"I don't think so," Pauline said. "He didn't hide her clothes. For me, that means he didn't kill her."

"It's suggestive," Steve said, "but not definitive."

They argued the point in a friendly fashion all through the drive back to Lithgow.

The end of the week saw Pauline back in her boss's office with a slim file on everything she'd found regarding the contract he'd signed. She felt her best plan was to let him read it without her providing any comment. It might have been her best plan, but it wasn't enough.

"Is this it?"

"Yes."

"When I signed it, I'm sure there was a letter with the

contract, outlining all the steps that had been taken to ensure the contract was sound," he said.

"According to the procedures, there would have been," Pauline said. "It isn't in any of the files I've been through."

"Have you had your staff looking?"

"No," Pauline said. "I thought it best not to make this widely known at this time."

"Hmm," her boss said. "Maybe, you're right." He sat silently staring at the few sheets of paper before him, thinking. Finally, he continued, "I don't see why they didn't approach me to save themselves when I called you in? With this, they would have had real leverage over me."

"That had occurred to me, as well," Pauline said. In fact, it was the one thought that had kept her thinking she would not be undermined by him. None of this had come out at the trial. Her boss wouldn't be here if it had, so either they'd tried to use it against him and he'd carried on with the investigation regardless or, for reasons not clear, they hadn't yet tried to use it.

He looked at her sharply, trying to gauge if her neutrality was honest or a test in some way. He must have decided it was honest because he said, "I can't think of any long game they could be playing, can you?"

"The only thing I thought was maybe they are planning an appeal based on you being the criminal and them only following orders. Their defense could have the offices raided by the police to find this as clear evidence."

"I heard they were planning an appeal," he said slowly. "What a mess."

"I still don't see why they didn't use it in their original trial though," Pauline said. "It would have been equally as powerful evidence against you then."

"It still puts me in a damned awkward position now," her

boss said. "I have to tell the board what we've found. They can't hear it from someone else."

"I think that would be best," Pauline said. "You also need to have an account of what you remember placed in the files -- my department's, and yours."

He nodded. "I'll write it today," he agreed, "if I can't find anything in my own files. Maybe there'll be more in them that will jog my memory. Damn them." He paused. "Listen...," he began, and paused.

Pauline froze, hoping desperately he wasn't going to offer a bribe or try to coerce her into hiding this. She liked him and wanted it to stay that way.

"Yes?"

"My time here may be limited," he said. "The next board meeting is two weeks away and all arranged. I don't think they'll want to bring the meeting forward so there's that time and they'll possibly want time after to consider what they heard. Even if they feel it best that I leave, they may want me to stay on until a replacement is found. Can you be finished in three weeks? I'd really like my legacy here to be a better something, even if it's just a stronger financial system."

The intimation her own position wouldn't long outlast his own, gave Pauline a sinking feeling inside. She'd hoped this would be a step up into the executive suite at home and, somewhat inconsequentially, she'd only just arrived and hadn't begun to explore the beautiful countryside around the town or seen any of the sights she'd put on her 'must-see' list.

"I can have the procedures finalized, rolled out, and have people start using them," she said. "Whether that will be enough to make them last beyond our time here, I can't tell."

He nodded. "You may have more time," he said. "A new

managing director may approve of this work. I'll do all I can to sell it to him. But new brooms like to sweep away old dust."

Pauline smiled. This was the second time recently she'd been called a new broom. "I'll pick up the pace," she said, "and plan to have it rolling out to the staff by the board meeting. You'll have what you remember about the contract ready for the files tomorrow?"

He nodded. "Yes," he said. "Tomorrow."

17

IDENTIFYING THE PRANKSTER

PAULINE ARRIVED BACK at the house, tired but hopeful. After her meeting with the MD, she'd immediately met with her managers and impressed them with the need to have the procedural changes completed in two weeks. She told them the boss wanted it so because he was to report to the board, and he wanted to re-assure the board the changes were well in hand. This wasn't entirely truthful but close enough. There had been little dissent and even, she thought, some enthusiasm for a challenging schedule that would inject life into a generally too regular office routine.

What to tell her housemates, the voices, was a different matter. She'd taken to talking to them whenever they appeared, and she also talked to the more unnerving presence in the bathroom. She felt it was good for her and for them. Unfortunately, she'd assured them she was going to clear up the matter that perturbed them so much and now that seemed unlikely. Perhaps she'd hold off telling them at all and just leave when her time was up. After all, they couldn't follow her, she thought, smiling.

After midnight, she was woken by another argument.

Just him and her. No child. The debate was heated but not, she felt, violent. She strained her ears to make sense of what was being said but, as always, she couldn't. They were speaking English; she recognized the flow and the sounds, but infuriatingly not the words.

"Why can't you be clearer?" she asked when her patience was running out. "What use is it to include me this way but leave me high and dry to your meaning?" She stuck her fingers in her ears. Yes, that worked. The voices were gone. She often tried this to re-assure herself they weren't just in her head, and she wasn't going mad. Finally, she slipped out of bed, grabbed the flashlight she kept on her bedside table for these midnight searches, and went once again to track down the source.

As always, she was unable to find any source but searching made it feel like she was doing something. The voices could be heard in many places throughout the house but not outside. She returned to bed with a final, "You'll be sorry when I'm gone," to her invisible tormentors and went to sleep.

WORK NOW WAS HECTIC, as old documents were replaced with new ones, staff were re-trained in the new ways, and her boss kept up a constant demand for updates. The effect of the change had put the detective's investigation almost out of her mind until he appeared beside her at the water station asking for a meeting.

Pauline said, "See my secretary. I'll have her pencil you in later today. Can you give me some idea what it's about?" This last was for the benefit of anyone who might be listening.

"It's a personal matter," Ventnor said. "Nothing serious but somewhat delicate."

"I'll make sure there's time today," Pauline said, walking away.

"What is it?" Pauline asked, the moment Ventnor sat down.

"I know who carried out those pranks and they're planning something new."

"Who and when?"

"You probably won't recognize the name," Ventnor said. "His name is Gareth Roberts, and he works in the factory stores. The changes your report set in motion screwed up a lot of people on the fiddle here apparently, not just the financial folks. He had gambling debts and was diverting storeroom supplies to pay for them. He got quite a beating when the good times ended. He lost a finger and his good looks. He blames you for that."

"How horrible," Pauline said, grimacing. "If he was a sensible man, he'd blame his own behavior for his troubles."

"If he was a sensible man," Ventnor said, grinning, "he wouldn't have had those troubles to begin with."

"You say he's going to try again?"

Ventnor nodded. "Yes, but I think he's even more bitter now. His lack of success at intimidating you seems to have unhinged him."

"What do you suggest?"

"I suggest alerting the police and having them guard you," Ventnor said.

"They won't have someone they can spare to shadow me," Pauline said.

"I agree. My second suggestion is you tell the police, and I will stay near but out of sight in their stead."

"You're not being paid for bodyguarding," Pauline said. "Are you sure you want to do this?"

"I'm an army reservist," Ventnor said, "and he's a nasty piece of work that needs a lesson. It will be a pleasure."

"He's already had one lesson," Pauline said. "That's what started this, you told me."

Ventnor grinned. "Some people are slow learners," he said.

"And you say it's soon?"

"That's what I've heard."

"Are you sure this man hasn't seen through your cover and is setting you up?" Pauline asked.

"It's a possibility, of course," Ventnor said, "which is why we need to have the police in on it."

"Very well," Pauline decided. "I'll call them now and you start shadowing me right after work. I have a pull-out couch bed in the living room you can use. How we get you into the house without being seen is the problem."

"After dark will work," Ventnor said. "We both work late, and I travel to your house lying down in the back of your car."

The plan worked well, though Ventnor had no clean clothes for work the next day. As they breakfasted together, Ventnor said, hesitantly, "Did you hear voices in your room?"

"I think the couple next door argues a lot," Pauline said. 'I do hear them sometimes. Did they wake you last night?"

He nodded. "I even went to the window and listened outside, but I couldn't hear anything there. It seemed all around me in the living room. Downright creepy, it felt."

Pauline laughed. "I thought it was just me," she said. "Some nights, they go on for hours."

"Well, tonight I'm going to tell them to shut up if they carry on like that again," Ventnor said, grinning. "It must be somewhere nearby, but I don't think it was the house right next door."

"Not next door to the room you were sleeping in, no," Pauline said. "That's Mrs. Creighton's house and she's old and widowed."

"Is it the prankster?" Ventnor asked. "Maybe, he's behind it."

"If it happens again tonight, you can find whoever it is and sort them out," Pauline said, smiling. Having searched so many times herself, she was confident he wouldn't find anything either.

Pauline woke around midnight, hearing stealthy movements in the living room. She smiled, guessing Ventnor had heard the voices and was going on a hunting trip. She wished him luck. Then she realized there were no voices. If he was hunting, it wasn't her mysterious voices he was after. She slipped out of bed and threw on her robe.

The room was dark but there was enough light from her electric alarm clock and the pale outline of the window through the curtains. She crept to the door and quickly stepped through it.

"Shh," Ventnor said, waving his arm to stop her movements.

Pauline stopped and listened. Outside she could hear furtive sounds. It could be an animal, or it could be a man, one with a grudge to settle. Now her eyes were adjusted, she could see Ventnor held a pistol in his hand. She wished she'd brought her own gun with her to Australia but had decided Customs, at each end of her trip, would likely object. As it was, she had nothing except maybe a kitchen knife if she could get to the kitchen without alerting whatever was outside.

Ventnor moved silently to the door that opened onto the garden. He really was very good at this, Pauline thought. Army training must be a real asset in detective work where violence may be a factor. The difficulty for him, she knew, would be in opening that door. It creaked and squealed. She would have it oiled tomorrow.

Her fears were confirmed when, judging the time to be right, Ventnor threw open the door and leapt out. The sound of heavy footsteps running at the side of the house had Pauline racing for the front door. By the time she wrenched it open, all that could be seen was a burly man disappearing over a garden fence three houses farther down the street. Ventnor joined her on the sidewalk watching their prey disappear.

"I could have shot him," Ventnor said, "but the police frown on that sort of thing when you aren't in any danger."

"Was it him?" Pauline asked.

"I would say so," Ventnor said. "Same height, same build, moved the same way but I could never swear it was him to a judge and jury."

"Unfortunately," Pauline said, "he now knows someone is staying with me and he won't come back here."

"He might," Ventnor said, "but I think you're right. Now he'll look for other opportunities."

"That only leaves driving to and from work, really," Pauline said. "And maybe when I'm shopping for groceries."

"Check your car before you get in it from now on," Ventnor said, "and don't leave the windows open. We have a lot of poisonous things here in Oz. You don't want any of them in your car."

Pauline laughed. "You don't need to tell me. I visited the Natural History Museum before I left Sydney on my last trip; it frightened the life out of me. I was glad I was flying home."

"Same with the house," Ventnor said, grinning. "Nothing left open. Most dangerous animals avoid people, but they get frightened if cornered. Stuck in an unfamiliar location with a human being is enough to get any creature defensive."

"You sound like you're on the side of the creatures, John," Pauline said, smiling.

"I am," he said. "I mean, I will kill anything that is going to harm someone but only then. I like wild animals of all kinds."

They returned to the house and their respective beds, where Pauline thought out her next steps. If the lunatic was this angry and this determined, her own best interests were either to get him locked up, which would be difficult, or take herself out of his reach. It seemed fate was calling time on her Australian trip in more ways than one. Maybe her new research colleague, Steve Larsen, could provide a solution. She'd leave work on time later and pay him a visit.

"I DON'T THINK I know the man you're talking about," Steve said, when she told him about her difficulty. "He might be new in town."

Pauline grinned. "New since you retired?" she asked.

"Well, yes," he said, "or at least he never came up in any local story in my last years on the paper."

"Is there a way I can get him off my case?" Pauline asked. "None of his troubles were really my fault."

Steve laughed. "You seem to have a somewhat naïve view

of human nature for such a worldly woman," he said. "People with a grudge can rarely be reasoned with."

"Then do you have any clever ideas?" Pauline asked. "If I caught him in the act of vandalizing my house or car would that be enough to get him locked up for a time?"

He shook his head. "They wouldn't lock him up for that," he said. "More likely he'd get a fine."

As this was what Ventnor had told her during their nighttime discussion, Pauline wasn't surprised.

"So, I just wait till he murders me," Pauline said, sarcastically.

"I'm sure the law wouldn't be any different in England," Steve said.

Pauline had to agree that was true.

"I'll be happy to escort you when you need to go out," Steve said. 'And you'll be safe enough at work, I imagine."

"Thank you," Pauline said, "and I may take you up on that offer occasionally, but I really can't go through the next weeks with you trailing along behind me."

He laughed. "I suppose not. Now, do you want to hear my news?"

"Of course, it's what I'm here for."

"Mrs. Langton has agreed to let us visit her and talk about her son and daughter-in-law. We can go any night this week."

"Tomorrow night," Pauline said. "I'll pick you up right after work and we'll drive straight there."

18

A MOTHER REMEMBERS

Next evening, Pauline, Steve, and Mrs. Langton were seated in the old woman's house in a quieter part of Katoomba, drinking tea.

"What is it you wanted to know?" the old woman asked, her bright eyes and quick movements belying her advanced years.

Pauline explained about the house and her interest in the case, leaving out the voices and the presence. She felt this would only upset the old lady.

"Seems a bit strange," Mrs. Langton said, "being interested in something that happened so long ago."

Pauline used her back-home-I-research-local-history story and, again, it seemed to be enough.

"Well," Mrs. Langton said, "where to start?"

"Maybe tell us a little about your son and daughter-in-law first," Pauline said. "That way we will get to know them as people rather than characters in a story."

The old woman nodded. "Very well," she said. "Bruce was a gentle boy who cared about things: animals, people, the state of the world. As a young man, he grew more," she hesitated, "manly, I suppose you might say though he was never girlish. I don't mean that." She stopped again. "What I mean is, as a teenager, he took to sports, rugby, and football, and he joined the Army Reserve, but he remained a gentle soul at heart."

"I have a brother like that," Pauline said. "He's a great one for horse-play but dotes on pets and they love him in return."

Mrs. Langton continued, "I thought Shelagh was a perfect match for him. She was quiet and gentle. In fact, I thought her a bit insipid, really, but ideal for a man like Bruce. They got on so well, it seemed a marriage made in heaven." She stopped again, frowning.

"What happened to change that?" Pauline asked.

"It's a terrible thing to say about a child but that's what it was," the old woman said. "You may have heard people say that parents with daughters divorce more than those with sons. I hadn't but when I experienced that child with her tantrums, she could scream for hours or hold her breath until she was blue in the face, I believed it. I'd never seen anything like that."

"Was there anything wrong with her? I mean did they have a doctor look at her?"

"Oh, yes," Mrs. Langton said. "They were always sure she was hurting in some way, and they tried specialists in Sydney when the local doctors found nothing wrong. They couldn't believe it was just the way the girl was."

"Then?" Pauline asked, for Mrs. Langton was gazing into the far distance again.

"One day," she said, waking from her reverie, "Bruce came to see us without Shelagh and the child. He said, there were rumors that Shelagh was seeing someone. He wanted advice."

"Had you heard that rumor?"

"No, we hadn't, and we told him so but, as he rightly pointed out, people wouldn't tell us any more than they would tell him."

"What advice did you give?" Pauline asked, feeling she may be getting to a turning point in the story.

"We advised him to talk to Shelagh," she said. "Maybe we, or Shelagh's mum, could take the child for a day so they could really talk."

"I heard that's what happened," Pauline said.

"It did but not right away," Mrs. Langton said. "It was some weeks later. By then Bruce had come to us again, saying things were growing worse. The child hated him, he was frightened of her, but Shelagh insisted he spend more time with the child. We repeated our offer to give them a break so they could talk, though I must tell you, we were frightened of her too. You've never seen such directed fury in something so small."

Pauline, who was used to holding and playing with her nephews and nieces, found this a hard story to understand. Yet she'd heard it now from more than one source.

Mrs. Langton gathered her thoughts and continued, "Next, we heard Shelagh's mum had taken the girl for a few days and Bruce and Shelagh were talking through their problems. That's what he said, when he called into our house after work. He was happier than we'd seen him for months."

"Did he think they were recovering?"

"I think he did," the old lady said, "but he said, 'early days, mum, early days' when I asked."

"Then?" Pauline asked, as Mrs. Langton had again lapsed into memories.

"Bruce came to the house. He asked if Shelagh was

there, or had we seen her? We hadn't and he told us she wasn't at home, and he was suspicious."

"We asked why. He said they'd had a bit of a setback that morning before he'd left for work. Now, the house was empty, and it looked like Shelagh had left early in the day. There were no lunch dishes or things like that. We said she was probably with her parents. He agreed and said he was driving straight there to find her."

"But she wasn't there," Pauline said.

The old lady shook her head. "Bruce was back around midnight and told us. We said, go to the police, which he did."

"They would want to wait, I imagine," Pauline said. "That's the law in Britain, anyway."

"And it is here," Mrs. Langton said. "They could do nothing until it was sure she hadn't just left Bruce. Bruce pleaded with them to reconsider. She wasn't with her parents, and she'd left her daughter, which a mother would never do. It did no good."

"Did you hear from Bruce while he waited?"

"He wasn't waiting," Mrs. Langton snapped. "He and his father began searching immediately. They visited work friends, colleagues, old school friends, everywhere Shelagh may have gone to. They found nothing."

"Then the police began organizing searches, I understand," Pauline said.

"Finally, yes, and they and the townsfolk searched for days. We all took part. Because Bruce had already visited the likely townspeople, the search immediately began in the surrounding country."

"There's a lot of dense bush out there," Pauline said. "I've only taken short walks from the parking areas, but I can see how hard it would be to find someone who'd become lost."

"We searched for days," Mrs. Langton continued, "and tried to get Bruce to come back with us at the end of the day but he wouldn't. He thought she would go straight home if she found her way out. We didn't like him going to his home alone because we could see he was brooding. He looked like death with the worry and the walking. We were hours out searching and he was first out in the morning and stayed to the end each day."

"Did you get the sense others were threatening him?" Pauline asked.

"Not threatening," the old lady said. "They were shunning him. People would walk past him without even saying a word. People he'd known since childhood. It made my husband very angry; I can tell you. I had to restrain him once or twice, reminding him it wouldn't help Bruce to have people even more riled up."

"It sounds horrible," Pauline said.

"It was. It's part of why we moved away when it was all over," Mrs. Langton said. "We couldn't forgive, you see."

"I can understand," Pauline said. She could see but could also understand the townspeople's suspicions.

"As the days went on," Mrs. Langton said, "it was clear to us Bruce wasn't eating. He'd lost a lot of weight and was as gray as a corpse. We urged him to come home, where I could at least get food into him. I brought him food to eat while we walked. He said he couldn't eat. After three days, I had to stop going on the searches. I was too drained. My husband continued for another day but even he found it too much. Then, a day later, the police came and told us Bruce was dead. He'd killed himself." She fell silent again, staring at a distant painful past only she could see.

Pauline let her recover before asking, "Did you believe that? That he'd killed himself, I mean?"

Mrs. Langton returned from her thoughts. "By then we'd thought he might, he looked so deathly. Still, we never believed he would you know. We were so confused. It wasn't a shock, you see, but we didn't think he really would. I can't explain it better than that."

Pauline nodded. There seemed nothing left to say.

"The coroner's verdict was suicide while the mind was disturbed," Mrs. Langton said. "His mind was certainly disturbed, and we found out in the days that followed why that was. Everyone had been whispering he'd killed Shelagh because she'd been having an affair. It was the first we'd heard this outrageous slander. We told people how Bruce and Shelagh had been recovering. They pretended to sympathize, but we felt their disbelief. It hurt my husband so badly, we had to leave."

"Is there anything you've heard since, that sheds more light on it?" Pauline asked.

"Not really," the old lady said. "Though we did hear there was a man Shelagh had been carrying on with after all."

"Do you know who?"

"Rumor said it was Fergus Drummond, but rumors aren't reliable, are they?" the old lady said.

"Not always," Pauline said, though in her mind she was thinking they generally were true. People were always quick to uncover salacious behavior. As a species, people seemed to home in on it at once. Part of that men-never-really-knowing-their-children-were-theirs worry that had led to so much unhappiness throughout time.

As they drove back to Lithgow, along the winding mountain road down from the top of the plateau to the valley below, Steve said, "Did you get anything new from that?"

"I got a better feel for Bruce," Pauline said. "I'm not sure there was anything really new, but hearing Fergus Drummond was Shelagh's lover might be," she paused, shook her head dismissively, and added, "though I suspect it was just more of the rumors we've been told about."

"I thought it interesting even his parents began to doubt his innocence by the end," Steve said.

"Yes," Pauline said slowly. "They began to doubt but were still angry enough to leave town so weren't totally convinced, I think."

"I think that shows they *were* convinced," Steve said.

"It always frightens me how easily people slide into a tragedy," Pauline said. "I don't yet know what happened here but I'm sure that there was a time when someone could have taken a different action, and all would have been well."

"Your optimistic view of human nature does you credit, Pauline," Steve said, grinning. "The old newshound in me says people behave badly and they know they're behaving badly. There's rarely a 'road to Damascus' conversion. More often it's a doubling down on what they're doing wrong."

Pauline smiled. "I'm not naïve," she said. "I know what you're saying but I'm talking about regular folks, not people in high places. Just ordinary Joes and Janes who get in over their heads."

"You may be right," Steve said, "but I think you'll find over the next few weeks that the Joes at least, aren't as cuddly as you would like them to be."

"You mean the contract talks?"

Steve nodded. "I do. It's always unpleasant but this time will be much worse because of the new environmental regulations and the new international free trade rules. This will be the start of years of fighting."

"It's already begun back home," Pauline said. "Coal miners demanded and got exorbitant wage rises during the oil embargo and then the government, who owns most of the mines in England, had to start closing mines that couldn't produce coal that could pay those rates."

"This is a mining and electricity producing town too," Steve said, "and the new environmental regulations are making them harder to sustain when we can buy goods from other places. You'll need to look out for yourself."

"I'm in finance," Pauline protested, "and here to introduce new ways of doing things. I'm not line management."

"Your last visit led to a lot of, shall we say, side businesses being curtailed," Steve said, "and it's finance departments that drive management to make hard decisions, so I don't think you'll escape the growing storm."

"My boss has already suggested much the same thing," Pauline said. "I only hope it isn't as bad as you both fear."

"It's bad in other places around the world," Steve said. "We see it on television news every night. Your countrymen back home are making quite a name for themselves. And providing an example for every hothead around the world to follow."

"I don't watch TV," Pauline said, "so I hadn't realized it was being spread everywhere."

"Not watching television is good for your mental health," Steve said, "but it can lead to blindness to the world around you."

"I'm afraid I think that's exactly the reverse," Pauline said. "What little I've seen has always struck me as manufactured and over-blown. Far from incidents being the major events they claim, they're usually very small."

Steve laughed. "You're talking to someone who made his living blowing small items into major scandals," he said, "so I agree with what you're saying in general. Still, you'd be surprised how a small incident, carefully managed, can turn into a giant disaster when copied elsewhere. Be careful, Pauline. The mood in town is ugly right now. That's all I'm saying."

"I will," Pauline said, "but I still have to work and live so I won't be running just yet. Now, who are we going to talk to tomorrow night?"

"An old man, older than Mrs. Langton," Steve said. "He'll explain why I began to consider foul play in respect to Bruce's death."

19

THE LOVER UNMASKED

WHILE PAULINE WAS EXCITED at the prospect of hearing from Steve's new witness, Mrs. Langton's revelation that Fergus Drummond was the one the rumor mill had settled on as Shelagh's lover had taken hold of her imagination. Mr. Drummond had kept that from her when they'd spoken earlier, and she wanted to know why that was. On her way home from work, she called into his office. His receptionist checked Mr. Drummond was free and then invited Pauline to go through.

After the customary greetings, Pauline dived straight in. "I can understand this might be painful, but could you tell me about your affair with Mrs. Langton?" she asked.

"Oh, you heard about that did you?" he said. "Well, it was painful for years after but that's long past now. She was going to leave him and marry me, but he found out somehow, I guess. Maybe she told him herself. Shelagh was a very honest, truthful woman. She hated the way we were behaving behind Bruce's back."

"You think he killed her?"

"Everybody thought so," he said. "I saw no reason to think different."

"And now?"

"I still think so," he said. "The reason we didn't find her body is he took the secret with him to his grave."

"Yes, I can see how that would be," Pauline said. "When did your relationship with Mrs. Langton begin?"

He frowned and fiddled with his wristwatch. Then he said, "I'm ashamed to say it began when she was married." He paused. "In fact, it was after she'd had her daughter. Shelagh was very low in spirits and one day, when we met in the street, I tried to lift her out of the blues she was in with some light chat. Just as a friend, you understand. She was pushing the baby in a buggy, I remember." He smiled sadly and fell silent.

"It was as simple as that?"

Drummond nodded. "Yes. She thanked me for making her laugh and we went on our way," he said, "but there she was, next day, as I was making my way out for lunch. Our office at the time was down that end of town where they lived, and you now live. We talked, she was happy again, and it became a daily event. One we both looked forward to." He fell silent, his eyes focused on a point far away in time and space.

"And it moved on from there," Pauline said.

Drummond nodded. "It just felt natural," he said. "It was as if we were meant for each other. We were soul mates," he held up his hand, "and I know everyone says that but it's the way it felt."

"And then?"

"And then it continued," he said. "She was married and had a child. She didn't want to hurt Bruce, she said, and the child needed her real father. Like I said, she was very honorable that way. I found it heartbreaking, having to see her only when he was at work and I could sneak away from the office, when what I wanted to do was marry her and have our own kids."

"This went on for two years though," Pauline said. "Surely, feeling that way, you must have tried to encourage her to leave her husband."

"Of course I did," he snapped. "I loved her." He stopped abruptly, pausing for a moment to calm himself. "When she disappeared, I wondered if she'd told Bruce and that is what led to her... disappearance." He ended quietly.

"Did you tell the police this at the time?"

"I did," he said, nodding. "I wanted him arrested and hanged for what he'd done."

"Are you still sure he did it?"

He nodded. "Who else had a motive? Now, though, with all the time that's past, the anger has faded. Now I just feel a huge sense of loss that never leaves me. I don't think of it as often as I used to but when it comes up, like now, it's still there."

"I'm sorry to cause you such pain," Pauline said.

He shook his head, as though shaking off the memories, and asked, "Why *are* you so interested, anyway?"

Pauline smiled. "When I'm not doing accounting, my hobby is local history," she said. "I'm often told I couldn't have found two duller ways of spending my life but there it is. They're tough jobs but someone has to do them."

"Are you planning to stay on here, then? I'd heard you only had a short contract at the factory. If that's the case, you might not have time to finish digging into this bit of local history because the people living here have never solved it in twenty years."

"That's because people have to move on, I find, and they

stop digging," Pauline said. "I understand that. In many of the local events I've researched, I've found that there comes a point when people just let it go. Other things come up and, no matter how upsetting the event was, it's overtaken in people's minds by new events. This one, I imagine, was the same."

"That's true," he said. "You can only care for so long and then you have to let go."

"Your love for Shelagh must have kept you hoping for longer than most," Pauline said. "Weren't you angry when others fell away?"

"I was in a strange position, Miss Riddell," he said. "My affair with Shelagh wasn't widely known and I kept it that way after the deaths. Like many traditional places, people here have strong views on what is right and what is wrong. It wouldn't have taken much for people to start blaming me for what happened. They couldn't blame me more than I blamed myself, but they could have hurt me more than I wanted. I felt guilty but I didn't want to be the next to disappear or anything like that."

"Would it have come to that?"

"No, I'm just giving an extreme example," he said. "I probably would just have been forced out of town because no one would do business with me. You see, I felt guilty but was afraid of retribution. Not very brave of me, I know."

"I do see," Pauline said. "Did you continue looking for Shelagh's body?"

"We all did for days but when Bruce killed himself our best hope of finding her was gone," he said. "The bush is still thick out there. Like others, I went on looking at weekends and vacation days for maybe a year. Then I realized there was no point. Wherever she is, it's no better or worse than if we brought her remains back to town and buried her here. She wasn't religious or anything so a proper Christian burial wouldn't have meant much to her."

"Her family may have wanted a place to grieve," Pauline said.

"That's true. Her family lived in Bathurst so she would have been buried there, I guess," he said. "You know, I think in the end, Shelagh guessed what might happen when she told Bruce and that's why she sent the kid off to her parents. It was for safekeeping."

"I've spoken to both mothers," Pauline said. "In fact, it was Mrs. Langton who told me about you."

"How did she find out?"

"Years later, someone told her the rumors," Pauline said, "but Bruce had told her of them at the time. The only thing new was your name as being the lover."

He frowned. "I hope the old woman hasn't told anyone else," he said. "It makes me a target of gossip or worse if she starts telling others."

"She hasn't told anyone in all these years," Pauline said. "I don't imagine she'll start now."

"Still," he said, his expression hardening, "she might tell someone who tells Evie, and that wouldn't be good."

Pauline thought it a good time to change the subject. "Do you remember during the search someone asking Bruce Langton to tell them where the body was so you could all go home?"

He shook his head. "Why? Does someone say that's what happened?"

"Yes, and that night Bruce Langton hanged himself."

"Wow," he said. "You've only been here a month or so and you know more about it than I do. No one told me that."

"I wonder who said it," Pauline said.

"Didn't the person who told you about it remember?" he asked.

"Unfortunately not," Pauline said.

"It was probably a sad, sick joke then," he said. "One no one wants to remember; particularly if it happened on the day he killed himself. A person would feel guilty about saying it or just laughing about it when someone else said it, I would think."

"Probably," Pauline said. "Was there anything about that time that struck you as odd? Maybe not at the time but later?"

He shook his head. "No," he said. "Everything seemed normal except Shelagh's disappearance and then Bruce's death."

"It couldn't have had anything to do with labor relations problems in town at the time, for example?"

"I wouldn't have thought so," he said. "Labor relations problems are fairly common in traditional industry towns like this one. Every time the union contracts are up for renegotiation, there's trouble. That year was the same as ever, but they've never led to murder, at least not yet." Then he added, grinning, "Though I've heard this year may be different."

"When we spoke a week or so ago," Pauline said, ignoring his pointed remark, "you never mentioned your affair with Shelagh. In fact, you dismissed the idea she would have been having one, as I recall."

He nodded. "I dismissed the idea because she wasn't having affairs with other men and I've kept silent on our love affair for so long now, it seems like betrayal to even speak of it to others."

Pauline thanked him for being so candid and left his office in deep thought. His answers, while sensible, seemed too good to be true, somehow. However, she thought wryly, the truth was she didn't like him and so anything he said, she had problems with.

20

MORE FRAGMENTS OF THE PAST

LATER THAT EVENING, Pauline and Steve met the witness Steve had found. The man, Arnold, was living in a residential home on the edge of town. He was frail, confined to a wheelchair and seemed confused by their visit.

"Don't you remember my visit yesterday?" Steve asked, when the nurse brought him into the room set aside for such meetings.

At first, it seemed the old man wasn't going to rally but then a brighter expression appeared on his face. "Of course, I do," he said in a fierce whisper. "You don't think I'm completely ga-ga, do you?"

Steve hurried to assure him no such thing had crossed his mind and introduced Pauline.

"You're the woman interested in the Langtons?" he said, without any trace of hostility or defensiveness, which was something new on this case where everyone seemed suspicious.

"I live in their old house now," Pauline said, "and the case intrigues me."

'Hmm," he said. "Sounds a bit creepy to me. Why would you want to know about something like that?"

Pauline repeated her local historian story and once again it seemed to be enough.

"Let sleeping dogs lie, I should say," the old man said. "Well, what is it you think I can tell you that others can't?"

"Steve said you'd heard things that suggested Bruce Langton's suicide may not have been a certainty," Pauline said. "That's the sort of local knowledge that doesn't appear in the printed records."

"Nor would it ever be likely to," the old man said. "It's just men shooting their mouths off without any real evidence. The police, and even the newspapers," he gestured toward Steve, "like more than just gossip."

"But you heard things that made you think there was more to the story?"

"I did," he said shortly.

"Do you remember who was talking?" Pauline asked.

"I can't remember what was for breakfast, nowadays," he said, "and anyway, it was just people talking, whispering, muttering. Lots of men and not just once. It seemed like half the town was in on it."

"Where did you hear them?"

"In the pub and the Legion, any drinking place where they congregated after the day's search. They were hot, scratched, bitten, and angry," he said.

"And what were they saying?" Pauline asked, when he didn't continue his train of thought.

"That something had to be done. The police would do nothing without a body because there'd be no proof of murder. That sort of thing."

"You didn't hear anyone actually saying they were going to do anything personally though?" Pauline asked.

"Are you crazy?" the old man said. "Even with a few beers in them they weren't going to threaten murder in such a public place. That would be daft."

"I suppose they wouldn't," Pauline agreed. "Though people do say silly things when they're drunk."

The old man's expression became knowing, sly, even. "But that's my point, woman," he said. "They didn't. If it was all talk, they would have said silly things. When they were so careful about their words, I knew there was real intent behind it."

"I see what you mean," Pauline said, and she did. But proving a negative was beyond even her considerable expertise. "Yes, I do see that."

Leaving the home, Steve once again asked Pauline if she felt she'd gained anything from the interview.

"Yes," she said, "and I see why he didn't go to the police and why you didn't either."

"I did actually. I told them at the time," Steve said. "But they said there was no evidence anyone was in the house that night other than Bruce himself and that was the end of it."

"Have we any more witnesses?" Pauline asked.

"Not that I know of," Steve said.

"I can't believe Shelagh didn't confide in someone," Pauline said. "Women do. We need to get back to Shelagh's mother and my neighbor, Mrs. Creighton. There will have been someone. I'm sure of it."

"Do you believe the two people we've heard from?" Steve asked.

Pauline laughed. "I listen to what I'm told," she said, "but my father always told me, 'believe half of what you see and nothing of what you hear'. To which I've since added, 'and nothing of what I read'."

Steve smiled. "I'm a newspaper writer," he said, "you can't expect me to let that pass without protest."

"Protest all you like," Pauline said. "I've been involved with so many things the papers have written about, and I've usually found it hard to recognize even the actual event, let alone the fictional story the writer wrapped around it."

"We have to make it something people want to read," Steve protested. "Otherwise, it won't be read, or even printed."

"You have to make it something that sells papers and advertising space and is within the ideological slant of the paper's owner," Pauline retorted. "Which is why, after I'd read the local paper's articles, I came to ask you about the events of the time. I hoped, with the passage of time and without a financial motive, I could learn something closer to the actual events."

"You may have a point," Steve said, "but I still take issue with your statement of 'nothing of which you read.' We rarely tell lies, even though we have to develop a story around the events."

"The point is, I don't want to wade through nonsense to get facts," Pauline said. "Now, you were there, you knew these people, who would Shelagh confide in?"

"There was a group of young people, they were the last kids born before the second war. They were at school together and then pairing off together," Steve said, his face screwed up in concentration. "Most of them have left the area now, I'm sure. Let me dig out some old files and see if a name jumps out. The difficulty is, I wasn't one of them. I was a middle-aged man to them, and they were just kids to me. I wasn't in their confidence, you understand."

Pauline nodded. "Do some digging, I'll ask Mrs. Creighton."

21

HER DETECTIVE LEAVES

Work the following day confirmed the fears Steve had shared the previous day. Although not directed particularly at her, Pauline could sense the tension in the hallways. Through her office window, she could see a shop steward haranguing the men in the yard at lunch time. Her heart sank when her secretary said John Ventnor had asked for a meeting.

"Did he say what about?" Pauline asked.

"He said it was personal."

"Bother," Pauline said. "He's probably going to quit on us just when we're getting him trained."

Her secretary hesitated before saying, "There's talk about him."

"What sort of talk?"

Again, the hesitation. "People think he's a management spy," she said at last. "It may be best for him if he is quitting."

"That's nonsense," Pauline said firmly, though she knew there was truth in it. Just not the truth the staff thought. "Well, if you're right," Pauline continued, "he may have been given the hint and that's what he's coming to say."

Ventnor was prompt to his time and shown straight into Pauline's office. He always looked stern and serious but today, even more so.

"What is it, John?" Pauline asked.

"You've seen the hotheads out there," he said, gesturing to the window.

"At lunchtime, yes," Pauline replied. "I hope you haven't come to tell me you're their leader and you're all going on strike."

He grinned. "No," he said. "I'm not the striking type. No, I'm afraid I've had some bad news from home and will have to leave today."

"Today?"

"Yes. It's an emergency and I need to be home in Sydney as soon as possible. I'm leaving on the 3:30 train."

"When will you be back?" Pauline asked. "We're on a tight schedule, as you know, and being a man down is a serious problem."

"I'm not sure when I'll be back," he said. He leaned forward and whispered, "And I don't think you'll make your schedule. There's a work-to-rule about to be announced so you won't get anything out of anybody until the contracts are settled."

Pauline's heart sank. Nothing was going right on this assignment. Would her boss even last until the contracts were settled? Would she be allowed to finish her work, or would the new contracts explicitly forbid the revised procedures? She couldn't help feeling, from the comments she'd heard, there were more people on the take than just the two finance executives they'd uncovered, and the unfortunate Gareth Roberts.

"Well, you must do what's best for you, John," she said, loudly enough for her secretary to hear. "Be sure you get your timesheets signed off before you go and hand back all the company's effects."

He nodded. "I will," he said loudly, and then softly, "unfortunately, I don't see a way for me to continue shadowing you. Shall I have the agency send someone new?"

Pauline considered, and then shook her head. "I'll talk to them about a replacement when we see how things are developing," she said.

Ventnor left the office and Pauline called in her secretary. "It seems you were right," she said. "Make sure Mr. Ventnor does whatever is required before he leaves."

When her secretary had gone, Pauline called her boss and asked to meet off-site. Somewhere they could talk privately. He suggested his house after work.

With this arranged, Pauline called in the manager who had been Ventnor's supervisor to re-arrange the work and plan how they might still meet their deadline. The MD would want to know she was still pressing forward with their reforms.

That evening, Pauline pulled into the drive of a Queensland-style home on the side of the valley overlooking Lithgow. A very pleasant spot today, though the view would have been hazy in the days when the blast furnace was in operation.

"Drink?" her boss asked when he'd ushered her into a quiet room away from the family.

"Sherry, if you have it," Pauline said.

"This is a bad business," he said, handing her a glass filled to the brim. "You'll have heard the rumors; I expect."

"I have and Ventnor told me before he left," Pauline said.

"I wish he'd been able to catch the prankster before this

began," her boss said. "I knew Ventnor would be suspected once the trouble started. I hoped we had another week or so."

"I suspect my changes to the procedures actually brought the trouble forward," Pauline said. She told him what she'd learned about Roberts and the factory stores and the potential that there were similar fiddles everywhere.

His expression was bleak. "When the men at the top are rotten, it goes right through the organization," he said. "As you know, I was brought in only a year or so ago because of the strangely poor performance of the Australian division. It took months for me to get a handle on it and to get you folks out to investigate. Now it looks like I'll be brought down with them."

"Surely the board will see you're making progress and stand by you," Pauline said.

He snorted. "They'll look for a scapegoat to avoid a shut-down," he said. "You'll see."

PAULINE DROVE BACK to the house in a somber frame of mind. Everything was unraveling too quickly, and she could see it ending without any success. She parked in the carport and instead of going into her house, strode around to Mrs. Creighton's house and knocked on the door.

There was the same interminable wait as last time but eventually the door opened, and the old lady peered around the edge, saying, "What do you want?"

"I wondered if you knew who Shelagh Langton might have confided in," Pauline said.

"Well, it wasn't me, if that's what you think."

"I'm sure it wasn't," Pauline said, trying not to sound

sarcastic. "It would be someone more her own age, I would think."

The old lady shook her head. "The only person I ever saw next door in those last months was that Drummond fellow. The one that has the office on Main Street."

Realizing she wasn't going to get anything more from the old lady, Pauline thanked her and left. Drummond had told her he was Bruce's friend and Shelagh's lover but not about visiting the house during the weeks leading up to the end. He'd suggested the opposite, in fact. Was that significant? She decided to challenge him on that as soon as possible. Getting information out of Fergus Drummond was like pulling hen's teeth, as the saying went.

22

THE PRANKSTER GETS PHYSICAL

PAULINE WAS WAKENED in the night by heavy rain drumming on the roof. It hadn't rained since she arrived. She was surprised how loud the noise was in her room. Used as she was to English slate roof tiles, she hadn't previously encountered the peculiar booming sound the downpour was creating on the house's thin metal roof. She slipped out of bed, put on a robe and went to look out the glass doors into the garden. As she did so, a bolt of lightning flashed across the sky, lighting the garden momentarily.

The sight of the rain pounding the lawn and trees was etched on her mind and with it, the shape of the man standing watching the house. She stepped away from the window, crossed quickly to the kitchen, slid a knife from the block and returned to the window. Once again, she wished she'd brought her automatic pistol on the trip, and she made a resolution to never travel without it again. Her self-defense training would be more than adequate against an opportunistic purse-snatcher, but this man had a grudge and wouldn't run off when she fought back.

When the next lightning flash lit the garden, however,

the figure was gone. Had he gone home or was he hiding nearby, waiting for her to fall asleep? The noise from the rain on the roof would give him an advantage if he was planning to enter the house. She could hardly hear herself think, never mind hear furtive attempts to open doors or windows. That decided her. She did an inspection of every door and window, ensuring they were solidly closed and locked before taking a cover from her bed into the living room. She stationed herself in a comfy armchair placed at the corner of the room with her back and sides protected by solid walls, and prepared to wait out the night.

For the morning shower, Pauline stood under a torrent of cold water trying to shock herself fully awake. Her head seemed stuffed with wool and her eyes felt full of grit. The usual oppressive feeling she experienced every time she showered crept over her but, tired and angry, she said, "Go away. I haven't time for you today!"

For a moment, she felt it had gone away but slowly it began again to envelope her and as always, she finished washing as quickly as she could.

As she drove to the police station to report her nighttime visitor, she once again wondered about that tin roof. Was there some way it played a part in the voices she heard? The roof was an amazing sounding board for the rain overnight, why not for quarrels beyond just her neighbors' houses? Or was she just looking for a rational explanation of events that she couldn't accept weren't rational.

The drive to work was slow, for the storm had washed out parts of the roadway. By quitting time, that had seemed an omen, for her workday was also a washout. No one was working on anything. She pointed out to her managers that the phrase 'working to the rules' still included the word 'work' and she expected them to make sure staff were doing some. By the time she left the office, she realized her assignment to this organization was never going to be done. She may as well tell the managing director tomorrow so he could find another crutch to support him at the board meeting. With that resolution made, she ran into him as they were leaving the office building. Pauline told him how things stood.

He frowned. "If I thought it could be done in time," he said, angrily, "I'd hire an agency to do all our finance from today and lay-off our present bunch of lay-abouts."

Pauline grinned. "I'd like to do that too," she said. "Today has made me so angry, I could murder them."

"With Ventnor gone, have you had any further trouble?" her boss asked.

Pauline related the events of the previous night.

"You have alerted the police, haven't you?"

"Of course, and they say they're cruising past my house more often on the afternoon and night shifts but beyond that, they can do very little," Pauline said.

"We have a spare room, if you'd prefer not to be alone," her boss offered.

"Thank you, that's kind, but I have other reasons for staying where I am." She explained about her research into the house and its history.

He grimaced. "That sounds like an even more compelling reason to move out," he said. "Surely you can't feel comfortable living in a house where a possible murder-suicide took place?"

"I don't suppose you lived here in Lithgow then, did you?" Pauline asked, ignoring his question. She didn't want to mention the voices or the presence. He was the sort of take-charge man who'd insist on protecting her.

"No, we're newcomers here," he said. "When I took up

this post it was the first time I'd even set foot in the state. I'm Queensland born-and-bred and so is my wife."

"Pity," Pauline said. "I'm not getting far with my local history research. So many people have moved away from the town since that time and those that remain don't seem to have been as close to the missing woman as they should have been."

"Our cleaning woman might know," her boss said, as they reached their cars, which with labor trouble brewing, were both being sheltered in the maintenance shop's lot. "She's local and she's probably the right age. I could ask her for you."

"Please do," Pauline said. "I need a break on this, and she may be the serendipitous contact that provides it."

On her way home, she called into Drummond's office. He was in, just preparing to leave.

"I think I told you everything I remember about that time," he said, when she explained her visit.

"I'm sure you did," Pauline said untruthfully. "It's just I haven't found anyone else who was as close to them as you were. I was hoping something may come to mind if we talked some more."

"I can't stay long," he said, "but ask questions and I'll do my best to answer."

"The last weeks before the tragedy, did you visit them at home?" Pauline asked. "Did you see or hear anything that might now seem important?"

"I visited once or twice but you couldn't hear anything in there for Evie screaming," he said. "That bothers me a bit now. I was told she was teething, but it went on and on for weeks and I don't see that with other kids. Anyhow, I stopped going."

"You were Bruce's friend; I think you said?"

"Well yes, but by then I knew both of them equally well," he said. "I was jealous of Bruce. Don't get me wrong, it wasn't just sexual jealousy. It was more he had a wonderful wife, kind and caring, and I was still single and hoping to persuade her to leave him for me."

"Did you never find anyone, afterwards, I mean?"

He frowned. "No," he said. "After Shelagh disappeared, I hoped for a long time, and then I think I lost interest. Anyway, it just never seemed to happen somehow," he said. "You know you really should speak to Evie. She was too young to remember, of course, but people will have talked to her about her parents, I'm sure."

"You know her well," Pauline said. "Could you make the introduction?"

"I'll do that," he said. "Call me tomorrow night and I'll let you know when."

Evie was an Abba fan. It wasn't hard to guess this; her whole outfit had been lifted from an Abba set. The skin-tight lycra pants allowed even the most casual observer to see she wasn't wearing any undies or, if she was, they were the thong-style. Both the pants and the peculiar top she was wearing shimmered in the sun as she approached the outdoor restaurant table where Pauline and Drummond were sitting.

He stood and kissed Evie's cheek in greeting before introducing Pauline, who held out her hand and was left looking foolish when Evie slumped in a chair and said, "I have places to be, make it quick."

Pauline looked at Drummond for guidance. His expression was one of embarrassment and he said, "Evie did say she could only spare a few minutes, but I thought it best for you to meet tonight and then you will know each other for follow-up questions."

"As I didn't know my parents," Evie said, interjecting, "we can do everything here and now. I wasn't there when it happened. They can't pin it on me." She laughed so Pauline would understand that was a joke.

Pauline's opinion of the woman, which hadn't been high, sank further. This heartless, tasteless joke about her parents, one of whom certainly died violently, was horrible. However, they were here together, and Evie may have some insights to give.

"I hoped you may have been told things about your parents, by their friends and colleagues, throughout your life," Pauline said.

"Hell no," Evie said. "Why would they?"

"I thought maybe you might have asked about them?"

"Why would I?"

"Curiosity, if nothing else," Pauline said, still finding it hard to believe anyone could be so callous.

Evie seemed to find the suggestion a puzzle, one she found hard to solve. After a moment of pretended thought, she said, "Nah, I never had any curiosity about them and no one spoke to me about them, 'cept my gran. She sometimes said I was nothing like them, by which I was to understand they were good people, and I wasn't."

"Everything I hear about them also says they were good people—" Pauline began but was stopped by Evie's mocking laughter.

"Good people," she cried. "He killed her and hanged himself." She went off in another burst of harsh laughter that sounded false to Pauline but could have been genuine. She didn't know the woman, after all.

"It's the gap between what I hear about them and the events I'm told about them, that puzzle me so much," Pauline said. "Doesn't it strike you as odd?"

Evie shook her head, her big hairdo staying surprisingly stiff as she did so. "Nah. My gran only said they were good so she could make me a sinner by comparison," she said. "But they couldn't have been good, could they? I'm their child and no one will tell you I'm good. You're way off there, lady."

Pauline struggled to maintain her composure against this foolish woman's words and said, "There's nothing you can think of that might explain what happened?"

"I don't know why you're asking me," Evie said, "Fergus here was their friend. He tells me often enough. Ask him." Her gesture toward Drummond was dismissive, contemptuous.

Drummond said, mildly, "I suggested Pauline meet with you in case you knew or remembered something I didn't, Evie. I've already told Pauline everything I remember."

"Then you're an idiot," Evie said, springing to her feet. "I've no interest in them now and I never have. They're dead and no use to anyone. They certainly didn't think of me when they were killing themselves. Why would I think of them?" She flounced off toward her car, her tightly clad buttocks appearing to wink at Pauline and Drummond as they watched her go.

"Evie doesn't seem to value the support you give her," Pauline said, allowing her anger to overcome her usual good manners. "Not even a goodbye."

"She's a moody kid," Drummond said, in a conciliatory tone. "Sometimes she gets upset. Maybe reminding her of her parents puts her on edge."

"Has she ever asked you about her parents? She knows you were their friend."

"No," he said, "she hasn't. I put it down to the sense of loss she must feel but I did think she might open up to another woman, if she thought something good would come of it."

Pauline thought she'd never seen anyone with less empathy or sense of loss in all her years of investigating but decided not to say so. Perhaps a lighter moment would help.

"Is Evie an ABBA fan?" Pauline asked. "She seems very taken with their clothes."

Drummond laughed. "She's on her way to an ABBA night at the Newnes Hotel," he said. "Haven't you seen the posters?"

Pauline shook her head. "I hadn't," she said. "ABBA are very big in Australia, I understand. They were touring when I was here last and to great acclaim, so we heard."

"You aren't a fan?"

"I like their songs," Pauline said. "They have melody and a sense of fun, which isn't something you can say for most popular music nowadays, but I'm not a fan, no."

"I'm not either," Drummond said. "You think a sense of fun, I think cheesy, which is why I'm *not* going to be there tonight."

"Well," Pauline said, rising from her chair, "thank you for helping me meet Evie. It didn't add anything new but maybe it did show me another person who has been injured by what happened, even if she doesn't realize it herself."

"That's what I think," Drummond said, rising alongside her. "I think she was damaged by her parents' death. It's part of why I help her, I suppose."

They parted company at their cars and Pauline drove away shaking her head at such apparent naivety. Drummond knew what Evie was like before the death of her parents and he imagines her present behavior is grief? Perhaps, she thought, some men grow sentimental as they age and become easily fooled. And what about the way they behaved toward each other. He helps her, Pauline had been told, but she didn't seem grateful, not even polite. Did she resent his help? Did he press her for more thanks than she was prepared to give? Whatever their relationship, it didn't seem cordial but maybe it was just a bad day. Either way, it left her with another dead end.

It was also another sunny evening fading into another warm, dry night, which was the perfect setting for the man who wanted to hurt her. She parked her car in the carport and went quickly into the house, bolting the door behind her.

23

PRANKSTER CAPTURED

THE NOISE of the door to the kitchen being rattled alerted Pauline immediately. She grabbed the phone she'd moved into her small defensive corner and, as quietly as she could, rang the police. It seemed to take a lifetime but finally the phone was answered. She quickly told the duty officer her stalker was about to enter the premises and added, "Don't come with flashing lights, sounding horns, sirens, bells, or klaxons. Drive here quietly and we'll get him for trespass if nothing else."

She heard the door open as she put down the handset. She'd deliberated long and hard about wedging this door shut, as she had with the others, for it might make him suspicious that it wasn't blocked. In the end, she'd decided she had to chance it. He had to come in and he had to come in where she could see him and where her defensive strong point would give her most protection. The knife was in hand and so was the water pistol she'd filled with liquid soap. Picking them up, she waited to see him walk into the room.

"Good evening, Mr. Roberts," Pauline said, as she saw

him silhouetted against the kitchen window. "I've been waiting for you."

He turned and his eyes searched for her in the darkness. Finally, he saw her standing in the corner of the room with walls and heavy furniture at each side. He could only approach from the front.

"And I've been waiting for you," he said. "Waiting to make you pay for what you did to me and all the poor people like me who have to get by the best way we can." He began to move slowly toward her.

"Don't come any closer," Pauline said. "We can talk well enough at this distance."

"It isn't talking I have in mind," he said. "I lost a finger, and I spent a week in hospital cos of you and you're going to feel some of my pain."

"You suffered because you're a criminal and your criminal friends are thugs, not because of anything I did," Pauline replied.

"It was a victimless crime," he said, still edging closer. "The rich can afford it. You made it a crime with a victim, me."

"Stay where you are, Mr. Roberts," Pauline said. "I'm not as helpless as you imagine." She brandished the knife and pistol so he could see them.

He stopped but then said, "I don't believe you'd use them. Your sort always leaves the rough stuff to others."

"*My* sort doesn't approve of rough stuff at all," Pauline said. "But we do approve of self-defense and that's what I can do. I promise."

He edged closer, clearly trying to determine if she was bluffing.

Pauline prayed the police would arrive in the next sixty seconds because that's how long she estimated she had before he summoned up the courage to spring upon her, and she was forced to stab him. It would be self-defense, but judges and juries were notoriously vague nowadays about what constituted reasonable force. She had no wish to have her remaining time in Australia spent in a prison cell.

"The police know you're here," she said. "At this moment, the only crimes you've committed are trespass, breaking and entering, and threatening behavior. Not so serious. If you attack me, you're looking at serious prison time."

He paused. "Can't hear any cars racing to your rescue," he growled. "You're bluffing."

The door was flung open with a crash and a voice said. "She's not."

Pauline breathed a sigh of relief but didn't take her eyes off Roberts until he was being led away.

"Your intervention was timely," Pauline said to the sergeant who was waiting behind to interview her. "He was about to jump; I could sense him stiffening his sinews."

"We were waiting for something a bit more criminal," the sergeant admitted. "With the charges we have, there's a good chance he'll get bail."

"Wonderful," Pauline said, sarcastically. "So, I can expect him back stalking me in a week or two."

"Sadly, even less than that probably, yes," the sergeant said. "Like I said, something more seriously criminal would have been better but he might have done you a lot of harm before we reached him. In the end, I thought it best to intervene when we did, particularly as you're waving around a knife. Judges and juries don't like victims who fight back. It muddies the water."

"I thought one of my problems was over and done with now he was in custody," Pauline said, inviting the sergeant to sit at the kitchen table so he could take notes. "Now it seems it isn't."

"You have more than one criminal problem?" the sergeant asked.

"Not necessarily criminal," Pauline said, "but serious, nonetheless. Now, what can I tell you so you can lay as many charges as possible?"

When she'd answered all his questions and added a lot of information he didn't ask for, she escorted him to the door and locked it behind him. With Roberts in custody for the night at least, she was about to leave it at that. Then she shook her head. No. If a lawyer had Roberts out on bail by morning, she needed to be in the habit of wedging the door shut. She may as well begin now. A kitchen chair under the door handle made it secure and she went to bed for the first sound sleep she'd had in days.

24

LABOR UNREST THREATENS A HALT TO EVERYTHING

Pauline called the meeting to order and surveyed her management team with a stern eye. She anticipated a difficult meeting with harsh words spoken and thought it best to start as she meant to go on.

"I want a report from each of you, verbally here in this meeting, and written later, stating how we're progressing with the revised financial procedures to ensure the integrity of the company's assets," she said. "The MD is meeting the board in a few days, and he needs to show we're moving in the right direction."

There was a general shifting in seats during this speech that didn't bode well.

"Andy?" Pauline said. Andrew MacDowell was always a straight talker and could be trusted not to hide the truth. She felt he would set the right tone.

"Progress is practically non-existent," he said, "as I'm sure you know. The work-to-rule makes it easy for all kinds of obstacles to be put in our way."

"Of course," Pauline said, "but it's our job to push for work to be done."

"And we do," MacDowell said, "but the men know our government has sold us out on these Free Trade deals and that our owners will sell us out as soon as they can get contracts negotiated with foreign companies. No one is fooled here; everyone can see from the TV news what's happening in all the western countries. The men know their jobs are gone and they'll soon be on the scrapheap. Naturally, they want as much as they can get out of the company before they're laid off."

"It sounds like you agree with them, Andy," Pauline said.

"I do because when the men are gone, we're gone. We'll be on the same scrapheap."

"Then I take it you're not pushing the men to finish?" Pauline asked.

"Then you take it wrong," MacDowell replied angrily. "Our only hope to continue on when the mine and power station close is for us to be running a tight ship. I'm telling my staff that if we can stop the pilfering from the stockroom up to the boardroom, maybe we can make our revenues last and hang on until we get new customers."

"Excellent," Pauline said, genuinely pleased. She liked old MacDowell and would have been sorry to fire him. "I hope the rest of you are finding similar arguments to motivate your staff?"

There was a mumble of agreement that Pauline was sure was unlikely to be true, but MacDowell had given them something to work with.

"Are your men responding to this argument?" one of the others asked MacDowell.

MacDowell grimaced. "Officially no," he said, "but I think I see some movement when the union steward isn't around."

"But how likely is it to be true," another asked. "Let's be

honest. For us to find new customers, we'd have to move the factory and offices to Sydney. We're too far out of the city to compete against companies on the spot."

"If we don't, we're dead," another said. "It will be hard to compete with cheap foreign wages but if we clean up our act, we have a slim chance, which is better than none at all."

A heated exchange of opinions followed this, and Pauline was forced to call the meeting to return to the agenda she'd set.

After the others had reported, Pauline dismissed them saying she wanted a written report by the following evening. A time frame she thought would give them a chance to work on their staff and report some glimmer of hope. It was a slender thread for her boss to take into a board meeting but the only one they could provide without outright lying. Meanwhile, she had another problem to work on and she meant to do that by dropping in on Steve Larsen on the way home.

"Pauline," Steve said, opening the door. "I'm glad you called in. We need to keep working if we're to get to the bottom of your murder mystery before you leave."

Pauline laughed. "I'm leaving, am I?"

He smiled. "So, I hear. Between Gareth Roberts stalking you and the union shutting down your new processes, you'll be on the next plane. Come in. We'll sit out in the garden to talk but talk quietly. Fences have ears around here."

With a hospitable glass of sherry (Steve had bought her favorite brand after their first meeting) Pauline explained the reason for her visit but somehow it didn't seem so pressing now, even to her ears. Work wasn't going to be a success, Roberts would be bailed and be twice as angry as he was before, and she almost certainly would be flying home very soon. Add to that it was a perfect summer evening. The sun was sinking down behind the encircling eucalyptus-covered mountains, shrouded with the blue haze that had given them their name, and the sky was turning gold, soon to be purple before nightfall; she felt she could just let it all go.

"Drummond," Steve said, answering her question, "is one of those men who is very active and busy. I'm sorry, that sounds uncharitable. It may be he's just active in so many things because he never married and he needs to have company. I can't say."

"But you don't like him?"

Steve frowned. "I think it's fair to say I don't like him, but I don't dislike him, if you understand me."

"Yes, there are people like that," Pauline said. "They seem to do everything right but somehow it just feels wrong. I suppose that's why I'm asking. He arranged for me to meet Evie Langton and the whole meeting was fraught with tension. She was angry, he was embarrassed, and neither were helpful. I can't see why he arranged the meeting when he must have known how she would take it."

Steve nodded. "He struggles with women," he said. "He doesn't get them at all. He probably *did* think Evie would want to talk about it and, as he helps her out with her expenses, she would be happy to go along with it. He wouldn't realize how angry that would make her, which is probably why he's never married."

"Give me some more background," Pauline said. "What sort of man is he?"

"He grew up here," Steve said. "He was one of the young people of the time when the events took place. Even then, he was a bit on the outside of social life. A hanger-on rather than a central character."

"He said he was more Bruce's friend than Shelagh's," Pauline said.

Steve nodded. "He would be. Like I said, not popular with the girls. He was already looking to succeed in business though."

"In what way?"

"As a teenager, he worked odd jobs and bought a parcel of land on the edge of town with his savings. He told everyone he was going to build his own house, and, over the years, he has. It's an impressive place."

"Can we drive past it?" Pauline asked. "You can talk while I drive."

"Why not," Steve said, grinning. "You should be safe to drive after only one glass of sherry."

Drummond's house was impressive, Pauline had to agree as they drove slowly along the dirt road that ran alongside the property. It resembled an American ranch-style building, all on one-level with a sun-facing verandah running the length of it.

"Did he build it himself?"

"He built the first cabin on the site," Steve said. "But as his business interests prospered, he's had architects and constructors build the one you see here. You can still see his first cabin among the gum trees at the back."

"I see it," Pauline said. "He must still use it for something. It looks decorated."

"I believe he uses it as a retreat. He's into meditation and other eastern practices."

"What are his business interests?" Pauline asked.

"Property from the start and now he owns a number of places in town," Steve said, "but it was his insurance agency that really set him up. When that did well, he could afford to expand the properties."

"Now he just lives off the rents, I imagine," Pauline said.

"Since he sold the insurance agency, probably," Steve said, "but he still buys and sell properties from his office on Main Street, and he consults on property development too. He does well."

"I've been to his office," Pauline said. "An all-round admirably entrepreneurial chap, in fact."

"He's certainly that," Steve replied, grinning. "He's also involved in charities and youth groups."

"I wonder how he finds the time," Pauline said, as she turned back onto Main Street heading back to Steve's house.

"Like I said, no family."

"He takes an interest in Evie Langton, that should give him a taste of family life," Pauline said, wryly. "She's still a rebellious teenager."

Steve's expression darkened. "There are rumors," he said, "and they're no more than that, which say his interest is more than charitable."

"Evie's grandmother said as much the day I spoke to her," Pauline said. "I didn't know how much weight to put on that because her grandmother's a very socially conservative woman. What do you think?"

"I stressed that these were rumors because I simply don't know," Steve said, "and I don't care to find out."

"They say history repeats itself," Pauline said. "Twenty years ago, there were rumors about her mother and now about Evie. It gives me a sense of déjà vu."

"I hope it doesn't end as badly," Steve said, somberly. "It needn't. She has plenty of male friends her own age so she's not reliant on him."

"Changing the subject a little," Pauline said, "What do

people say about his business practices? He has a contract with us that seems very generous."

"I didn't hear that," Steve said, grinning. "If what you say is true, I guess it would be for the influence he wields. They say he's the power behind the throne, at the town and regional councils. A finger in every pie. He would be a useful person to have available, even if the rate seems high."

"I see," Pauline said. "That would make sense, though I don't know of any projects the company was about to embark on that would need his particular expertise."

"They may have been pushed back or canceled before you arrived here," Steve said.

"You've given me a lot to think about," Pauline said, as she dropped him off and prepared to drive home. "Could you get Drummond to give us a tour of his property?"

"Oh, he'd be happy to show us around," Steve said. "He's proud of it and he's right to be. He's a genuine local success story."

"Then ask him," Pauline said. "He's one of the few people left from the time of the events and I'd like to know more about him. I think he knows more than he says, or maybe more than he knows he knows, perhaps."

"Okay, but don't forget, we still might find people to interview," Steve called out, as Pauline pulled away.

Pauline's thoughts, however, were too focused on the coming night. Throughout the day, she'd argued back and forth in her mind whether the voices she heard in the house were maybe just Gareth Roberts all along. After all, the harm she'd inadvertently done him occurred after her previous work at the company and, on hearing she was returning, he might have been stalking her from the start. The voices may well be human and not ethereal after all. If so, tonight would be a good test.

Once she was indoors and the doors were locked and wedged shut, she called the police station to inquire if Roberts was still in the cells. He was but he was due in court tomorrow and would be requesting bail.

Pauline hung up the phone and said in a firm voice to the spirits of the place that she still didn't believe existed, "You have tonight to prove to me you are real." She felt rather than heard the sigh. Was it weariness, sadness, or disappointment? Like everything about the voices, it was there but indecipherable.

As the evening grew quiet, road noise died away, the birds settled for the night, and the lamps came on, she heard the faintest murmur of conversation. A man and woman talking, far away and yet, as always, right here in the room with her. They sounded defeated. No longer arguing or discussing, just resigned to their fate.

Pauline shook herself. This was silly. She had no idea what they were saying or what they were feeling. She was imagining everything.

"I'm still here," she said, just to hear a real voice. "I won't give up." The voices fell silent, but she felt they were re-assured rather than driven away. More imaginings, she thought grinning wryly; it's me that needs re-assurance.

She settled in bed with her new book, *The Thorn Birds*, an Australian novel that had become a worldwide hit. She'd also bought the newest James Herriot, *All Things Wise and Wonderful* to remind her of home in the Yorkshire Dales but first she wanted to immerse herself in Australia's rural life, so *The Thorn Birds* was her reading for the next days.

The doings on the fictional farm of Drogheda had a lot of similarities to Pauline's own early life on her parents' Yorkshire farm and she was well immersed in the story before she heard them. Softly, the voices crept out of the shadows in the now darkened room and were soon all around her. It was as if the man was on one side of her bed and the woman on the other. A steady murmuring that could not be ignored. Putting a bookmark between the pages, Pauline placed the book on her side table, grabbed the flashlight, so she could see into dark corners, and set out to investigate once again. Tonight's search was to be different from her previous ones. Tonight, she wanted to see if Roberts had left a tape recording with a speaker somewhere. Until recently, she'd never considered such a prosaic solution. With him in custody, it couldn't be him speaking. Either he'd left a recording behind on a speaker or there really were voices in this house.

She started in the bedroom, where she could use the room's lights to search, before moving to the living room where she'd heard them earlier. After an hour, she drew a deep breath and began to search the bathroom. She hated this room and would have left it entirely out of the search, only she knew she had to do everything if it took all night. There was nothing. The voices were in the air, not behind walls, furniture, or any of the house's fittings. That only left outside, which she would do during daylight. She returned to bed, set the alarm for dawn, and tried to sleep.

She was wakened by the alarm, which was a shock for she was sure she hadn't even closed her eyes. She rose, splashed water on her face, dressed quickly, and set off to scour every inch of the outside walls. At the end of an hour, she'd found nothing but two snakes and an odd rattish sort of creature that hopped away like a tiny kangaroo. It looked harmless, much more so than the snakes, but she'd ask about it at work for it appeared to live at the house as much as she did and it clearly resented being chased away.

Showering after her time spent among the shrubs and

grasses was a necessary and, as always, uncomfortable experience. The room emanated cold in a land that was hot. By the time she was washed, dried, and dressed for work, she was sure in her mind that the noises had nothing to do with Roberts or tape recordings. Her newly formulated solution to the peculiar occurrences was wrong, as so often happened in her investigation of mysteries.

Worse was to follow. Later that day, she heard from Inspector Halleck that Roberts had been released on bail. That evening, before she locked up for the night, she called on her neighbor, Penny, and explained the situation. Penny was outraged and agreed to watch Pauline's house for any burly men who might be on the prowl.

25

MORE TROUBLE AT WORK

Work remained tense but she thought she'd grown used to it now, until her secretary asked through the partition if she would take a call from the factory manager. Pauline said she would and picked up the phone when the call was put through.

"Mr. Goodall, what can I do for you?" Pauline asked as cheerfully as she could. This call, the first ever from that side of the plant, would not be good news.

"You can get a directive from the MD about which set of rules govern the stores right now," he said, grimly.

"I don't understand," Pauline said. "What has finance to do with the stores?"

"The workers and foremen in the stores are being trained on the new rules around managing our stocks of materials and tools," Goodall said in a deceptively gentle tone. "And, as everyone is working to the rules, and they haven't been clearly told when the rules switch over from the old to the new, they won't release anything to the shop floor."

Roberts, Pauline thought angrily. That man is becoming

insufferable. However, she knew she'd never be able to prove he was behind this stoppage, so she contented herself with saying, "The changeover date is clearly spelled out in the training and in the documents, as you well know. However, I'll get a memo to the MD in the time it takes me to write it."

"I'll tell him it's coming and to sign it," Goodall said. "I'm going to see him now. I expect to see you there."

The phone slammed down before Pauline could say anything further. She called her secretary in, dictated a simple one paragraph statement of when the accounting changes concerning the management of materials and tools would begin, and waited while her secretary typed it into an official finance department memo.

"I'll be with the boss if anyone's looking for me," Pauline said and headed off for the MD's office.

Goodall was still in the MD's office when Pauline arrived. His expression was thunderous.

"Pauline," her boss said. "You have something for me to sign, I believe."

She handed over the memo, he read it, and signed it. Handing it to Goodall, he said, "Have my secretary make copies for you and the other managers and leave me the original." Goodall grabbed the paper and left without saying a word.

"He thinks we're as much to blame for the present state of affairs as any government rules," her boss said.

"It is a bad time to be reforming a company that's been running for years, admittedly," Pauline said. "Not only are people comfortable with their present way of doing things, but they're also unhappy at what we uncovered. Many, I'm sure, feel it reflects badly on them."

"It does reflect badly on them," her boss said. "The criminals who were caught were aided and abetted by others who saw what was happening and said nothing or, worse, took a share of the loot."

Pauline nodded. "You saw the connection between today's trouble in the stores and where the man who's been playing malicious pranks on me works?" she asked.

He nodded. "I wish we could have found evidence he did any of those pranks on company property," he said. "As it is, what he does in his private life isn't a justification for firing him in the eyes of the union. We'd have a full-scale strike on our hands."

"I'm not sure that wouldn't be better," Pauline said. "We could replace every financial operating document while they were all outside and they'd come back to find the work done."

"They'd make us jump through hoops training them before they'd use them," her boss said. "It sounds like a sensible solution, but it would be a nightmare when they came back to work."

The phone rang and her boss picked it up. He listened and then said, "Okay, let them but I want them back at work after lunch." He replaced the handset.

"That was Goodall," he said. "The steward is taking the stores' workers to a meeting where he'll read out the directive. The meeting, with questions and answers, he says will last until noon."

Pauline shook her head. What was the point in trying to run companies in a land where people found every excuse not to work? She could see why businesses everywhere in the west were already moving production abroad. That trend would only get worse as the western workforces reacted badly to every necessary change. She saw a very dark future ahead.

After lunch, Pauline walked out of the offices into the yard. Slowly, she heard machines starting and the sound of work once again thrumming through the factory walls. Metal was being cut, ground, milled, and welded. The factory was producing, though at what cost, only an accountant could really tell. She walked on, smiling wryly.

26

A REPRIEVE

THE DAY of the board meeting arrived, and Pauline was at work early, in case her boss needed anything new to take with him. They'd spent the previous afternoon and evening going through the progress being made until he was word perfect in his presentation. There was no call from the board room, so Pauline waited nervously all morning in her office, unwilling to leave the phone in case it rang. Her boss had said he'd call or drop by her office after the meeting and let her know their joint fates.

Time ticked away. Everyone in her department left for the day and time crawled by even more slowly than it had before. Finally, she saw her boss arriving at her office door.

"Well," Pauline asked. "Do we still have our jobs?"

He laughed. "Straight to the point, I see," he said. "That's what I like about you."

Pauline waited. When he didn't continue but sat in a chair across from her, she was about to ask again when he spoke.

"We're both safe for some weeks," he said. "We're to

finish our respective reforms and they will decide at that time."

"In fact, they'll use us as scapegoats for the turmoil that the contract negotiations will create," Pauline said.

He nodded, and replied, "More correctly like whipping boy and girl, I think."

Pauline was angry. Her career looked like it was over just as she'd really stepped onto the highest rungs of the ladder.

"We'll never recover from this, will we?" she said bitterly.

"The people who matter will know what happened," her boss said. "It's part of the game. Don't overreact. Keep your head down, get the work finished, demonstrate you've done what you were brought here to do, and you'll be okay. Trust me. This isn't my first time at this dance."

Pauline found it hard to accept what he was saying but she bit back the words and nodded. "I'll trust your judgment on this," she said.

"Talk to your people back in England tonight," he said, "and they can contact me if they want confirmation. Now, go home and enjoy some of our glorious summer weather. I bet you don't see much of this where you come from."

Pauline smiled. "I found the winter here too hot and sunny," she said. "If I stayed, summers would take me years of acclimatizing, believe me."

"Then perhaps what's happening is all for the best," he teased her.

"Of course, it's not for the best," Pauline snapped. "Going should be my decision, not others." She grinned. "Sorry, that was just silly, but I find this hard to take. I came here to do good, and I'll be sent home as a sacrificed lamb."

"Remember, we used to sacrifice lambs because they were a symbol of innocence and, yes, goodness," he said. "Trust me, this won't hurt your career."

"Easy for you to say," Pauline retorted. "You've already made it."

He laughed and left her office, wishing her a cheerful goodnight. Pauline wasn't sure she was ready to be cheerful, but his confidence sustained her on her drive back to town where she found Steve Larsen waiting on her porch.

"You must have something important to tell me," Pauline said as she locked her car.

"I have," he replied. "One of my friends from long ago moved away and we lost touch. I've been searching for a way to contact him and today, I learned his phone number. I called him. He remembers the Langtons well and he's happy to share what he remembers. I thought we could call him together tonight."

Pauline agreed they should.

"Follow me home and we'll call right away," Steve said. "I should have brought his number with me, but I forgot."

Pauline laughed. "I'll be there in an hour," she said. "I want to eat, change, and freshen up before I do anything."

"Don't be too long," Steve said as he walked back to his car.

Pauline was at his house before the hour was up. Steve dialed the number, which was picked up almost at once.

"Gord," Steve said, "me again. I have Pauline Riddell with me. As I told you, she's researching the Langton case and would love to hear what your recollections of that time were."

He handed the phone to Pauline, who introduced herself and outlined her story. Gord listened and, after general remarks of welcome, said, "You've probably heard everything I can tell you but ask away."

"You were friends with the Langtons, I understand," Pauline said.

"I was. I went out with Shelagh for a time when we were in high school, and I knew Bruce very well. We were in the Army Cadets and later the Reserves together."

"What do you think happened?"

"I think Shelagh was killed by a vagrant and Bruce killed himself," Gord said.

Pauline was surprised. "No one else has mentioned a vagrant," she said. "Why do you think that?"

"No one else would have done it," Gord said. "No one disliked either of them. They were really nice, and good, people. It had to be someone from outside."

"Were there vagrants in town at the time? Were any of them questioned?"

"Not that I heard of," Gord said. "But it wasn't at that time I realized it must have been someone passing through. It was later. My guess is someone grabbed her, perhaps not meaning to kill her but when they realized they'd done just that, they kept driving and buried her body miles from Lithgow in the bush. As I say, I thought about this a lot later and realized it was the only way it could have happened. We searched every inch of the bush around town and found nothing and the police searched the Langton's house and garden. It's the only thing that makes sense."

"Yes, I see that," Pauline said. "Did you hear the rumors about Shelagh that others have mentioned?"

"I did but that was rubbish. She wasn't that sort of girl," Gord said firmly.

"Was anyone mentioned in the rumors you heard? The name of the man?"

"I heard more than one name," Gord said, "which is why I knew it was garbage."

"Do you remember any of them?"

"They were all our high school or work friends," Gord

said. "The only one that was a bit odd was Fergus Drummond."

"Why was he odd?"

Gord laughed. "He got tongue-tied whenever a woman was about and would have run a mile if any woman had propositioned him. We all suspected he was a bit of a Nancy boy, to be honest."

"You'd rule him out as a lover, then?"

"Of a woman, yes."

"Do you remember anything that might shed light on what happened?"

"Not really," he said, "and me and the missus moved away soon after, so it all went out of my head after a time."

"If you do think of anything," Pauline said, "please phone Steve and let him know. I'd like to get to the bottom of this. It would help so many people."

"I don't see how," Gord said, "but, sure, I'll think on it and if I think of anything I'll let you know."

"Your wife can't remember anything? She must be around Shelagh's age, isn't she?"

"We talked about it after Steve called," Gord replied, "and no, there's nothing."

Pauline thanked him and handed the phone back to Steve who closed out the call.

"Anything?" Steve asked.

"Two things," Pauline said. "The possibility of a stranger, which no one else has mentioned, and the possibility that Drummond is homosexual."

"Some people did suggest a stranger, but it was never much considered seriously and then Bruce killed himself, which clinched it."

"But he didn't leave a suicide note," Pauline said, "which must have caused the police some doubt, I would think."

"If it did, they never mentioned it. They did search the house thoroughly, as you know, but beyond that, I think it was case closed. Even if it's still an open file somewhere in the records."

"And Drummond?"

"He's had some lady friends over the years," Steve said, slowly, "but it's true he never married. Maybe there's something in that."

"I'm heading home," Pauline said. "I want to ask the police about Roberts. He's out on bail now and I need to tell them to be ready if he tries anything."

"You don't believe he'd really harm you," Steve said. "Do you?"

Pauline related her experiences with the man to date and Steve offered to sleep over at her house, if she wanted support.

"Thanks," she said. "It may come to that but right now I want him to continue with his foolish behavior so we can get him put away."

Pauline called the police station to remind them of their promise of additional sweeps past her house during the night. Then locked, bolted, barred, and wedged every access point to the house before settling herself into her carefully placed armchair.

27

A SHOCKING DISCOVERY

THE FOLLOWING day at the office, when everyone was on their lunch break, there was a discreet tap on her office door.

"Come in," she called, looking up from the memo she was drafting for typing. Evan Morgan, who she'd barely spoken to since her early request for information, came in and closed the door behind him. Evan was a quiet, reserved man who rarely spoke in meetings or even in the corridor, so far as she could tell.

"I hope I'm not bothering you," he said, his expression troubled.

Pauline put his obvious discomfort down to him having some unpleasant message to deliver from the staff or his fear of being seen talking to her during the work-to-rule.

"Not at all," she said. "Take a seat."

He shook his head. "I won't, thank you," he said quietly. "What I have to say won't take long."

He's been sent by others; Pauline was sure of it now.

His expression was both puzzled and troubled by turns as he struggled with what he'd come to say.

"Yes?" Pauline asked.

"I know you're still investigating the Langton family tragedy," he said and stopped. Pauline waited.

"You probably know what I have to say already but maybe you don't," he said at last.

"What might I know?" Pauline asked, beginning to be irritated.

"You didn't see me the other night when you were driving in your car with Steve Larsen," he said. 'I was walking along the street."

Pauline waited as patiently as she could.

"He might have told you this," Evan said and stopped.

"Who might have told me what?"

"Larsen," Evan said. "He might have told you there were rumors he and Shelagh Langton were more than just friends."

Pauline was stunned. No. Steve had not told her that.

"Are you sure?" she asked.

"I'm not sure they were more than just friends," he said, "but I'm sure there were rumors to that effect. I thought you should know."

"Thank you," Pauline said. "Is there anything else I should know?"

He was puzzled. "I don't know what you know," he said. "I think I told you everything I know but... but then I saw you with Mr. Larsen and that triggered my memory."

"Will you tell me again what you remember of that time? That would help."

He shook his head. "The fellas will be coming back soon, and I don't want to be seen here."

"Then write it down and drop it off at the old Langton house," Pauline said. "As soon as you can."

That was agreed and Evan left, leaving Pauline

perturbed. She'd more or less accepted Steve's offer to have him stay over and now she'd discovered he'd withheld evidence from the time of the tragedy; evidence that may point to him as a suspect. She really had to be more careful who she formed alliances with in the future. And she needed to re-interview everyone she'd talked to, particularly anyone she'd talked to in Steve's presence.

28

RE-TRACING HER STEPS

THAT EVENING, Pauline found the phone number of Shelagh's mother and called Mrs. Brown. Who was surprised, and suspicious Pauline was calling again and said so.

"Since we spoke, I've talked to other people and I'm going back to all the people I spoke with earlier. Maybe my new information might jog some memories," Pauline explained. Her explanation seemed to be acceptable because Mrs. Brown told her to continue.

"For example," Pauline said, "I heard from one person that there were rumors about Steve Larsen and Shelagh. Did you hear that?"

"What does Steve say about that?"

"He hasn't said anything about it," Pauline said. "After all, usually the person the rumors are about don't hear about what's being said, do they."

"Probably not," the old woman agreed. "It doesn't matter anyway," she continued. "I didn't hear any of the rumors either. I'd have torn a strip off anybody who shared them with me, which is probably why I can't answer your question."

"Did you ever hear of the possibility of a vagrant being involved in Shelagh's disappearance?"

There was silence for a moment and then the old woman said, "I did hear something of that, but it was madness. Shelagh wouldn't have gone anywhere with a man she didn't know. She wasn't like that."

"It's possible she didn't have a choice," Pauline suggested. "She may have been forcibly abducted."

"I suppose that is possible, but a vagrant wouldn't have been able to get far with a struggling woman in tow."

"I think using the term vagrant is misleading you here," Pauline said. "I mean someone driving through town. A traveler of some sort. Not someone on walkabout."

"Ah, I see," the woman said. "That would explain her disappearance better. I don't think it was seriously considered. Maybe, if Bruce hadn't killed himself, it would have been. His suicide brought an end to it, really."

"I sense that from what I keep hearing," Pauline said, "and I think that's at the root of the difficulty for so many people. His death being used to confirm Shelagh's, I mean."

"To be honest," the old woman said, "like a lot of people, I thought she might come back when she heard he was gone. I suspect the police did too."

"Was the marriage a violent one?" Pauline asked. "Is that why you thought that?"

"I never heard it was and Shelagh didn't say so. Only that they were having terrible arguments over the baby and its continuous crying and Bruce staying late at work to avoid it."

"Not physically violent then," Pauline said. "Would Shelagh have found Bruce yelling at her abusive?"

"She was such a gentle soul," Mrs. Brown said, "I expect she would. But to be honest, Bruce was also a gentle man and I expect he'd be hurt at Shelagh yelling at him. I don't think either of them were up to the task of bringing up that girl."

"Yet you managed," Pauline said.

"Barely, and it estranged my husband and me too," she said sadly. "We were never the same again, even after she left our house. We should've put her into care once we knew Shelagh wasn't coming back."

"I met Eve a few days ago," Pauline said. "She seemed genuinely angry with me and with Mr. Drummond who'd arranged the meeting."

"She's always angry," the old woman said. "It's her normal way of being. I'm sure there's an illness there but I'm not a mental health expert."

"Does what I've said about the traveling man and the rumors jog any memories?"

"None at all," the woman said. "You have to understand, we were here in Bathurst when all this was happening in Lithgow. Our involvement was as outsiders, except for my husband and the searches."

"Did you offer rewards for information? Anything of that sort?"

"We posted notices in the Sydney papers; I remember now. At least, my husband did. The only replies we got were people who knew nothing, but wanted money, and cranks, who were very unpleasant."

"Well, thank you for speaking with me again," Pauline said. "I know this must be painful for you." She hung up and made notes of what she'd heard.

Soon after, Pauline heard the mail flap on the door open and shut and went to find an envelope on the mat. She opened it and found the promised statement from Evan Morgan. It confirmed everything she'd already been told with only that one small extra piece; rumors had linked Steve Larsen with Shelagh.

Now she thought about things with her eyes opened. It wasn't just Fergus Drummond who'd never married, Steve Larsen hadn't either. Pauline wondered if, as the saying went, Steve had been carrying a torch for Shelagh all these years? If so, did *he* know where she was buried? First, she had to know if he had a car, or access to a car, all those years ago. It opened a whole new possible avenue that she'd been blind to.

Next day at work, Pauline asked her secretary for the phone number of Mrs. Langton in Katoomba. The moment she had it, Pauline called.

Mrs. Langton was equally suspicious of her asking about Steve Larsen and his possible involvement with Shelagh. Like Mrs. Brown, she hadn't heard any rumors until after the events and couldn't remember any of them being about Steve, who everyone knew was a nice man and wouldn't have been the subject of such gossip.

"But he was a single man," Pauline said, "and that gives rise to speculation in these cases."

"Not that I heard," Mrs. Langton said, shortly.

"What about a possible traveling man abducting Shelagh," Pauline said, changing what appeared to be a touchy subject. "Was that ever mentioned?"

"I don't think so," Mrs. Langton said, "but as Bruce's mother, I'm not sure people would want to share their wild theories with me."

"I quite see that," Pauline said. "Does any of this awaken any new memories? Did you and Mr. Langton or Bruce post rewards for information, for example?"

"No," Mrs. Langton said. "There wasn't time. She disappeared and a few days later Bruce killed himself. For us, that was the end of it."

"Did you speak to Shelagh's parents about the child?" Pauline asked.

"We did, once," Mrs. Langton said. "They wanted us to take her part of the time, but it would never have worked. Children need a consistent home. Anyway, my husband wouldn't have had her in the house. That child was perpetually screaming, nothing pacified her."

"I heard that," Pauline said. "I find it hard to understand that a child would behave like this from the moment it was born. I know some parents allow their children to become tyrants, but this isn't the case here."

"We didn't understand either," Mrs. Langton said, "and I fear we made it even harder for Bruce and Shelagh by telling them they weren't dealing with the child properly. We thought they were too soft, giving in to her too easily."

"Later you changed your mind?"

"Over those first years we saw that it wasn't the parents at all. It really was the child. There'd been a film around that time called *The Bad Seed* and that's what she was – and still is, I hear."

Pauline thanked her for her help and hung up. As she should have guessed, the parents of the two dead people would have been out of the rumor loop and the person she needed to talk to was Arnold, the old man in the nursing home. She asked her secretary for that number and called immediately, knowing she was now being as dishonest with the company's assets as any of the people she'd investigated. At this point, she didn't care. She had invited a suspect into her home and her confidence, and she needed answers fast.

Residents, she was told, could have visitors before the

evening meal. She arranged a meeting with Arnold for late afternoon.

Pauline arrived early; such was her impatience for an answer to the dangerous situation she may have placed herself in. Arnold, however, was as scatter-brained as he'd been the first time and it took a lot of coaxing to get anything out of him. Finally, as she was about to give up and leave, he said, "One thing I heard you might like to know, young woman. That man you were with, Steve somebody. They say he was one of her lovers."

"Do you remember any others?"

"Other what?" he asked, bemused.

"Lovers."

"What lovers? I don't think you're right in the head young woman. Be gone."

Pauline took her leave and drove home, deep in thought. Did Arnold say what he said because she'd planted the idea in his head or was it a real memory? She was still musing as she drove slowly along Lithgow's main street when a loud thump startled her, and she slammed on the brakes. She was about to jump out of the car when she saw Roberts standing on the sidewalk, grinning, holding a bag of groceries and tossing an apple in his right hand, ready to throw it. She drove away quickly, parked in her drive, ran in the house, and barricaded the doors against the night.

That night, as she lay slumped against the pillows in her makeshift fort dozing fitfully, the voices drifted in and out. In broken, disjointed dreams, she saw Bruce and Shelagh. They were young, their faces pleasant, ordinary. They were shy at having their photos taken, that was clear, but their gentle natures were in their expressions. The old photos she'd been shown by their parents, and the wedding photo from the Mercury, didn't do them justice. Later, the dreams shifted. They were now old before their time, gaunt and gray with worry lines that hid their earlier light. They looked past each other, not wanting to see what each had become.

A pounding on the side door woke her with a start. She knew at once it was Roberts; it was still too dark for respectable visitors. Pauline stayed silent. He was probably drunk, full of that courage alcohol gives inadequate people. He'd grow frightened soon enough when neighboring house lights came on. Her patience was rewarded, for soon she heard a police siren wailing, growing louder and the hammering stopped.

She answered the doorbell a few moments later and gave the waiting police officer her version of the night's events. When he left, promising to spend more time on this street over the remaining hours of darkness, Pauline went to her bed. She'd have no more earthly visitors tonight; she was sure of that.

During the days that followed, she and her managers continued pressing their own staff to finish the procedures and, as individual ones were approved, began training other staff on how they were to be implemented. This was harder. In her own department, the managers could influence staff. But trying to influence managers of other departments to see a brighter future was hard. The prevailing belief was the mines and power station would go and then they'd be gone. They saw little hope.

As one older man said, "Our own government sold out the blast furnaces for cheap foreign iron all those years ago. They're doing the same with us now. You think we'll survive? You're dreaming. We're for the chop. You'll see."

The story of what happened to the valley's iron industry fifty years before was so well-known, and so well ingrained into the people, it was like pushing on a locked and barred door to get beyond it.

One evening, when she was at home, the phone rang. It would be Steve, she was sure. She wanted him kept at arm's length until she could be certain he was safe. If she'd learned he hadn't had access to a car all those years ago, that would have helped but she'd called in at the Mercury office and, with very little research, confirmed he did have a car at the time in question. Processing this additional information was causing her some heartache. She liked him and worse, she'd trusted him when she should have considered him a suspect right from the moment they met.

Pauline considered letting the phone ring, but she knew she'd have to speak to him sooner or later. She rose, crossed the floor to her corner fortress where the phone now permanently lived and picked up the handset.

"Hello," she said.

"Pauline, it's Steve. I finally got Drummond to invite us to his property. He suggests next Tuesday evening. I said yes. Is that okay?"

"Of course," Pauline replied. "Why don't I pick you up at six? Your place is closer than mine." In her own car, and with the short distance from his home to Drummond's, she felt she would be safe enough.

"Great," he said. "I'll see you then." He hung up.

Pauline considered her options. First, she needed to tell someone where she was going that evening and second, have her own unpatented self-defense pack of pepper and other non-lethal weapons in her purse.

29

DRESSING UP AGAIN

Pauline's office phone rang. She was puzzled. Normally her secretary warned her of incoming calls. She stood to look through the glass. Her secretary wasn't at her desk. Gone to powder her nose, Pauline thought, smiling at the old-fashioned phrase. She picked up the phone.

"Yes?" she said. There was silence. Had she taken too long, and the person had rung off in annoyance? She thought not. She shrugged and replaced the handset.

The phone rang. Pauline picked it up. "Yes?" Silence again. She placed the handset on her desk and walked quickly to her office door. Whoever was calling knew her secretary was away so they must be able to see her office and that should mean Pauline could see them.

What she saw was little more than a momentary glimpse of a burly shoulder disappearing quickly along a corridor away from her department. She practically ran to the far wall where she hoped to see him before he exited the door out of the department. All she saw was the door closing behind him. She returned to her office and called security.

The manager there assured her they would have

someone look into the incident and place a discreet watch on the corridor that connected the factory to the offices. It was the best they could do. This was really tending toward a police matter.

Pauline spoke to her boss, telling him about the incident and security's promise of additional surveillance.

"I'm growing tired of this," her boss said. "Can you be sure it was this man, Roberts?"

"No, I can't," Pauline said, remembering her unhappiness when she'd pointed a finger at Anthea Hobson, and Anthea had been found to be innocent. "We have to draw him out into the open somehow."

"Set a trap, you mean?"

"Yes," Pauline said. "He's attacked my car and my office. Maybe it's time to give him a shot at the real prize?"

"Absolutely not," her boss said. "This is a workplace, not a movie set."

As that was what Pauline had expected to hear, she wasn't dismayed. It just meant she had to carry out her plans away from work. With luck, it would wrap up all her investigations in one neat bow for, despite what Steve Larsen had told her at the start, Roberts was *not* a newcomer to Lithgow. He'd been a boy, but not a child, when Shelagh had disappeared, and he'd lived right here in town. She was sure now his peculiarly pointed revenge against her was not just because he'd lost out on a source of income but because he knew something about Shelagh Langton's disappearance, and it was both these motives that made him so persistent.

She called into the police station on her way home and spoke to Inspector Halleck, who was as unhappy at her suggestion as her boss had been.

"I can't allow that, Miss Riddell," he said, seriously.

"What you're suggesting is little more than entrapment and that's illegal."

"I'm not asking you to organize events," Pauline said. "Just be there when the time comes to act."

"But you are asking us to be part of a dangerous scheme to entrap this man doing something violent, which we both know he's capable of doing."

"If you'd held off a moment or two longer last time—" Pauline began but was cut off peremptorily.

"No!" Halleck said. "We will not be party to this."

"Very well," Pauline said, turning to go. "I'll catch him myself." She hadn't yet thought how she would do that, but saying it was necessary to force Halleck's hand.

"Miss Riddell," Inspector Halleck said. "This man could seriously injure or even kill you."

"I'm used to people trying to kill me," Pauline said. "You'd be surprised how many attempts on my life I've survived."

She could tell from his incredulous expression he didn't believe her, but she could also see he was beginning to accept she meant what she said.

"How do you plan to avoid being killed?" he asked.

Pauline described her leather coat, dog collar, and riding helmet outfit from a previous episode.

"Are you mad?" he said. 'That could never work."

"Well, it did," Pauline replied. "I think there is better armor nowadays though. I hear today there are vests made of something called Kevlar."

He considered for a moment. "We could give you one of those and a neck guard. We have helmets too."

Pauline shook her head. "I couldn't hide a helmet under a summer hat, but the body armor would be nice. Thank you."

"I'm not agreeing to schemes to entrap Roberts," Halleck said, "only offering you some protective clothing in case he attacks you while he's out on bail. You do understand that?"

"Certainly, I do," Pauline said, "and I'm very grateful. After all, it's neither of our faults the law has chosen to let loose someone who bears me such ill will. I don't feel safe with him loose. You are setting my mind at rest with this kind offer, it's a great relief to me." She thought she was laying the gratitude on a bit too thick, but it really was necessary.

Halleck led her to the police stores at the rear of the building and, with some difficulty, they found equipment that, while being too big, was at least manageable for her to wear. She left the station carrying her new clothes and planned how, when, and where she would actually wear them.

30

ROBERTS' LAST THROW OF THE DICE

She reached home and unlocked her front door, her arms filled with her new clothes. Her nose was immediately assailed by the pungent smell of dog waste. She pushed the door further open with her toe and saw, on the doormat, a mound of waste, collected and fed through the mail slot.

Pauline stepped over the mess and closed the door behind her. Dumping her body armor on a chair, she found a pail and shovel. Wrapping a towel over her mouth and nose, she scooped up the mess into the pail and carried it outside, throwing it into the bushes at the back of the garden. At least there, it would do good instead of harm.

The door and floor she scrubbed with bleach and the mat went into the washing machine on the longest possible cycle, with extra soap. At this point, she didn't much care if the machine foamed all over the kitchen so long as it washed out every scrap of dirt from the mat.

With that done, she marched into the bathroom and showered, saying angrily to her omnipresent presence, "Don't bother me tonight or you'll regret it." At that moment, she felt she could take on wrongdoing in every one of the astral planes and she'd be happy to do it. The presence, however, was simply there, reminding her but not pushing itself forward. Well, Pauline thought, with a grin, that's the way I'm going to approach all my showers from now on.

After a hastily eaten sandwich, Pauline spent the evening working on blending her Kevlar clothes into her regular clothes. It wasn't easy. The color of the Kevlar jacket was bright yellow and hard to hide under summer clothes. Worse, even when it could be hidden, it made her look at least twenty pounds heavier than she was. Her previous use of makeshift armor had occurred in winter where bulky clothes hid a multitude of sins. Australian summer dresses hid very little, as she'd discovered early on; only several petticoats underneath could make Pauline happy to leave the house in one.

Her work clothes were better. They were English suits of tweed and well-lined. By removing the lining, she finally arrived at a look that wasn't too odd. The neck guard was also bulky, and it took several tries with head scarves to come to a satisfactory arrangement. Looking in the mirror, she decided she didn't look like someone armored against angry men, just someone who was peculiarly susceptible to the cold in a scorching hot climate. It couldn't be helped. If she wore nothing but underclothes underneath, she might get through an hour wearing all this without swooning from heat exhaustion.

The sound of the voices grew while Pauline was finalizing her armor. She'd recovered her temper since the shower, so she only said, "And I wanted to come to Australia for the better weather!" She laughed at the absurdity of it all, the voices, the malicious prankster, and her ridiculous investigation of a two decade's old crime, one or all of which now necessitated her dressing up like an English maiden aunt at a summer garden party.

When she was to wear this was a problem. Obviously not at work. People would see it and in daylight recognize what she was wearing. Word would get around and Roberts would soon know. The evening walk from the office building to the car, however, may be a place she should wear the armor, which meant changing in her office after everyone left. Similarly, it would be imperative on her visits to the shops or library or church. Those were places she visited often and at a regular time. The perfect time for an attack.

To complete her armor, she needed another riding cap that she could build into a large summer hat. That was the only piece that she felt could be made to look sensible, for outdoors she already wore a wide-brimmed hat to prevent her pale skin from being burned. Luckily, in a rural area, there was no shortage of riding gear and she'd buy a hat tomorrow. Now, how was she to invite the attack so she was ready when it came? That was a puzzle she'd spend a disturbed night thinking on.

The answer came quite quickly as she ignored the voices mumbling just outside her hearing. Her most regular activity, and the one where she was most formally dressed, so her unusual attire would not look so out-of-place, was her visit to morning service at church each Sunday. Now, how to entice him into foolishness? That was trickier. Perhaps, if she transferred her devotions to Evensong, when the streets would be quieter, and dusk would be well advanced when she walked home, she could draw him in. She'd start on the coming Sunday. If he was stalking her as she was sure he was, his recklessness would do the rest.

31

TRAILING A COAT

SUNDAY WAS A LONG TIME COMING. There were no more unpleasant incidents to greet her at her house, for the police and her neighbors were now keeping close watch on the property. And the 'empty air' phone calls at work could no longer happen because, before her secretary went away from her desk, she blocked incoming calls. Pauline hoped this narrowing of his options would encourage the final mistake on his part. The police were alerted of her planned attendance at Evensong and the route she would use going to and returning from the service.

Work was slow for her now. The procedures were complete and the roll-out to the staff ongoing, which left little for her to do except field questions and complaints, while explaining the purpose to the unwilling recipients of her department's work. At each talk, she used Andy MacDowell's defense of what they were doing, hoping to get the staff to see there was benefit that might even save their future employment.

Saturday morning, she went shopping in her full suit of armor, hoping it looked like she was just popping in for groceries on her way to a royal garden party, as one does. She was surprised how little notice people took of her. She was sure she'd have been the subject of stares and whispers but apparently women shopping in tweed suits, neck scarves and floppy hats were common here.

She packed her bags in the car, all the while scanning the lot for Roberts. He didn't seem to be around, which was reassuring and disappointing. She thought the supermarket parking area too busy a place for an attack, even a so-called accident, but she'd hoped to see him following her, so she could be sure he'd be there Sunday evening when she was ready.

In the afternoon, she took the car and drove slowly along the narrow roads that pierced every valley, hoping she'd find she was being followed. She wasn't, which took away some of the pleasure she had in scanning the country, imagining the searches two decades ago. Her final destination, after visiting photo stops along the way, was Katoomba and the famous Three Sisters rock formation.

She'd visited them on her previous trip after the audit but wanted to improve on her photos and take the old miner's rail carriage down into Jamieson Valley where a trail led to the bottom of a waterfall. Pauline watched carefully as she locked up her car and walked to the railway ticket office. No Roberts. Again, she was thankful because it meant she could enjoy an afternoon sightseeing without being molested, but also disappointed because, if he didn't watch her closely, he may not learn of her change to the Evensong service.

"I should have sent him an anonymous letter outlining my arrangements," she muttered crossly to herself, after she'd bought her ticket and was waiting for the rail car to arrive at the top of a perilously steep drop. It arrived, and she and the others who were heading for the valley floor climbed aboard. The view down the rail to the valley bottom made her insides flutter but there was no time to change her mind. The open topped car began its descent at an alarming rate, which at least meant the trip was mercifully short.

The valley bottom was cool and shady, with a leafy canopy above to filter the sun. Pauline was thankful for that because her armor was beginning to make her perspire. 'Glow' her mother would say with a laugh, only gentlemen 'perspire'. Whatever it was called, Pauline didn't approve of it, so the shade was welcome. The crowd of holidaymakers who'd left the carriage with her soon dispersed along the trails. She was glad about that too. They were in shorts, T-shirts and flip-flops while she was muffled in her tweed suit, scarf, and sensible walking shoes that protected her ankles. She looked out-of-place and it bothered her a lot. Her concern Roberts would follow her and attack in some lonely spot had left her unsuitably dressed for the sunshine above. She did wonder about the other visitors' footwear. Hadn't they been to Sydney's Natural History Museum and seen how many poisonous snakes inhabited this land? Or did they know that they weren't in any danger; it was just the museum trying to make their exhibits seem exciting?

She followed the trail to the foot of Katoomba Falls and took photos of the rainbows that danced in the thin spray. The falls were barely running now summer was well advanced, though they must have been dramatic after the recent storm. At the edge of the stream that ran from the falls out into the valley, the plants were green and fresh, which made Pauline realize that, even under the overhead canopy along the trail, the ground had been dry. Every dead leaf, twig or piece of discarded bark had crackled underfoot. No wonder Australia was famous for wildfires when, even here in a dense forest with a stream, the undergrowth was like tinder. She retraced her steps to the rail, pondering the merits of a sunburned country versus a green and pleasant land.

After her day's sightseeing, Pauline was glad to change into lighter, more comfortable clothes. She'd barely finished her evening meal when the doorbell rang. She approached the door with caution only to see the figure of her neighbor through the frosted glass.

"Hello," Pauline said, when she opened the door, "come in."

"I can't stop," Penny said. "It's the kids' bedtime. I only came to say a man was here today, a burly, mean-looking man. I'm sure it was the one you told me to look out for. He was right here at your door. I told him you were out and asked if I could take a message."

"It sounds like him," Pauline said. "Did he say anything?"

"Just that he'd come back when you were home," Penny said. "I didn't like the way he said that. You should call the police."

"Oh, they know," Pauline said. "With luck, they will have seen him here too."

"There was a police car around but before this man arrived."

"He probably watched them go by before approaching the house," Pauline said. "It's like a game. He knows the police and I are watching for him, and he thinks he's being clever slithering around when our backs are turned."

"Some game," Penny said, grimacing, as she turned to go. "Be careful tonight. Scream loudly if you need our help."

"Thanks, I will," Pauline said, and closed the door. *So, he's still hunting for the moment to make his move*, Pauline thought as she returned to her evening sherry, her special treat of the day. He must have risen too late to see her leave and that's why he hadn't followed her into the bush. *Here's hoping tomorrow is where we catch him, and I wrap up my two mysteries in one unpleasant villain.*

"Do you hear my thoughts as I seem to hear yours?" she said conversationally to the empty room for the voices hadn't yet made an appearance. "If you do, hear this. With luck, this time tomorrow, I will have the answers you want of me."

She'd hoped this would spark a response, but it didn't. The room remained silent. Pauline shrugged and sipped her drink, running through all the possible ways she could be attacked tomorrow and how she would deal with them. Her self-defense lessons had stressed how important it was to be prepared for anything once you've become aware of a threatening situation. Her biggest concern was he'd try the hit-and-run with a vehicle kind of accident. Her armor wasn't proof against that.

Pauline woke with a start. The voices were shockingly loud tonight. Red light flickered on the walls of her room. Vaguely, she thought she hadn't seen that before when the smell of smoke jolted her wide awake.

She leapt out of bed and ran to the window. Pushing aside the curtain she could see firemen in the garden, lit by the flames she now realized were coming from the kitchen area. Pauline dressed hurriedly, unwilling to climb out of the window wearing only a thin nightdress. By the time she had on a skirt and blouse, one of the men was trying to open her bedroom window. She returned to it, pushed away the curtains and unlocked it. It still wouldn't open.

The room was becoming unbearable, smoke was creeping

down from the ceiling and the air was thick with the taste of burning. Her safety training from work had taught her not to open a door that had a fire on the other side, so she had no choice but to leave through this window. Unfortunately, as she also knew, breaking the glass would make it dangerous for her to climb out. The fireman at the other side, however, had no such concerns. He waved her away from the window, showing her the ram he would use to break the glass and frame.

Pauline stepped back, covering her mouth and nose with her sleeve for the smoke was making her gag. The window burst inward with a crash of breaking wood and the tinkling of falling glass, the flying shards appearing as flashing stars or dancing fireflies in the garish light. Once the broken edges had been smashed away, a thick mat was thrown over the window ledge and Pauline was signaled to climb out. Gingerly, she threw one leg over the mat and two men manhandled her out, keeping the rest of her body away from the remaining edges of the frame.

"Thank you," Pauline said, when they carried her far enough away from the house to be safe. "I'm all right to walk now." They placed her on her feet but held her arms until she'd demonstrated she was able to stand upright. "Another minute or two," she said, "and I'd have been carried out of there."

They grinned and left her, returning to the hose they'd dropped when they'd spotted her at the window.

Pauline watched as the fire was brought under control. The kitchen side of the house was badly damaged, but the rest looked as if she could continue living in it. She was glad for that. No sooner had she thought this when she wondered if she'd left on an appliance. Is that what happened?

When the fire was out, the fire chief and Inspector Halleck approached her.

"You won't be able to stay here tonight, Miss Riddell," Halleck said. "I'll leave an officer to guard against looters, but you'll need to stay somewhere else until the fire service is sure the house is safe, and we and they have identified the source of the fire."

"If my car is all right," Pauline said. "I'll go to the motel."

"Your car seems untouched," the fire chief said. "We got here in time to stop the fire spreading beyond the kitchen. Did you perhaps leave the oven on?"

"I didn't have the oven on," Pauline said. "It was too hot for cooking. And I always unplug the kettle after I use it. I'm very careful that way. Childhood training," she added with a smile.

"What about the washing machine?" he asked.

Pauline shook her head. "Not last evening," she said.

'My men have noticed the doors and windows are all locked and wedged shut," the fire chief said. "Have you had intruders?"

Pauline looked at Inspector Halleck, who explained the disturbances that had led to Pauline's precautions.

The fire chief nodded thoughtfully. "We should look at arson then," he said.

"You should indeed," Pauline replied. "Though how anything could have been introduced into the kitchen from outside, I can't explain."

"If it's there, we'll find it," he said and left to begin the search for clues.

"I won't keep you, Miss Riddell," Halleck said. "We can talk in the morning when we have a better idea of what happened. This may yet just be something as simple as an electrical fault. However, I will have one of my officers drive you in your car to the motel and stay outside your room door until morning." He held up his hand to silence the objection Pauline was preparing to make. "That wasn't a suggestion, Miss Riddell. You're in no state to drive and if this was a failed murder attempt, there won't be another on my patch."

As Pauline's legs did feel unsteady and she wasn't sure the motel would welcome a guest who arrived at one o'clock in the morning, unkempt, smelling of smoke, and without someone to vouch for their good character, she nodded and followed the police constable Halleck instructed to drive her.

32

IT WASN'T ROBERTS

Next morning, after an undisturbed sleep, a shower, and a hearty breakfast – being burned out made one hungry – Pauline drove back to her house. There were still investigators and firemen at the scene and a bored policeman who recognized her and wished her good morning.

"Good morning, constable," Pauline said. "Have they found anything helpful?"

"Yes," he replied, grinning, "but you'll have to ask the inspector what. I've strict orders to say nothing to anyone."

"Can I get any of my things?" Pauline asked.

The officer asked the firemen in charge who said Pauline could follow him. She was not to go in alone.

Pauline packed herself a small case of clothes and a soap bag with toiletries before looping her body armor over her arm.

"You may not need them anymore," the constable said as she exited the building.

"You got him?" she asked.

"I couldn't say," he replied.

Pauline threw everything in her car and drove to the

police station, where she was promptly shown into Inspector Halleck's office.

"Well?" Pauline demanded.

"Good morning, Miss Riddell," he replied. "I'm pleased to see you're none the worse for your experience."

"Did you find evidence of arson, and can you link it to Roberts?" she said, too excited to spend time on trivialities.

"Yes, to both," he said. "We have Mr. Roberts in custody, though he denies any involvement. The evidence says otherwise."

"Then I want you to also consider that he had a hand in Shelagh Langton's disappearance as well."

He frowned. "One thing at a time, Miss Riddell," he said. "I want to be sure we have him securely held on the arson charge before we go fishing for old crimes."

"I understand," Pauline said, "and I don't have any evidence to say he was involved in the earlier crime but there has to be something more here than just my work that's driving him."

"No evidence?" Halleck said.

"None," Pauline said, "and he would be quite young, ten or eleven maybe, but I'm almost certain he's the one."

"Because of all that's happened to you," Halleck said, seriously, "I'll have someone look at the possibility while we process the current charges. However, just so you know, allegations without evidence aren't something I like to hear, either as a person or as a police officer, and this is the second time you've done just that."

"And I feel the same way, Inspector, believe me," Pauline said. "But there must be more to this. There has to be."

She left the station almost happy. Roberts would not be bailed this time and they would find something to tie him to the events of twenty years ago. She knew it. Even better, there was still time to go to morning service, sans body armor.

Her optimism, however, was dashed when the following day she called Inspector Halleck from work to ask about progress.

"The good news," he said, "is no one is willing to post bail for Roberts. Our evidence that he's a danger to the public, or one member of the public anyway, is too compelling. We've also applied for a mental assessment of him, which has been granted. I think we may be able to get him put away for even longer, just in a mental home rather than a prison."

"But what about the Langton case connection?" Pauline asked. Her amusement at Halleck always teasing her by putting off answering her questions was wearing thin.

"There, I'm afraid, we have only bad news," Halleck said. "Your women's intuition has let you down, I'm afraid. He was in a juvenile detention center at the time of those events. It seems he's never been really stable, right from the time he was a child."

"You're sure about that?" Pauline cried, ignoring his dig at her deductive reasoning.

"We're sure, Miss Riddell," Halleck said. "When my officer returned with his findings, I sent him back to check further. I knew you wouldn't accept it."

"Then it's just his mental state," Pauline said, deflated, "and not a fear of being found out at last."

"That's about it," Halleck said. "Maybe now you'll let other professionals do their jobs and stick to doing yours."

Pauline bit her tongue. There was no point getting his back up at this time. She still may need him when she finally identified the culprit. Then she'd make him eat his words. For now, she could only smile and thank him for his advice.

"Well," she said, "thank you for letting me know. Can I move back into the house now? The rental office say they will have repairs done by tomorrow."

"From the police point of view, you can move back in anytime," Halleck said.

Pauline hung up the phone and considered her next steps. Work was ending. The passive-aggressive resistance to her new measures was slowly being replaced by acceptance that something needed to be done. The knowledge that senior managers and lowly storeroom workers had been stealing everyone's efforts for years had finally broken through. These weren't 'victimless crimes' as Roberts had claimed. Everyone who worked in the offices now felt they were a victim because the losses had come from the time they'd spent at work, from their own potential pay raises, from their own pensions, and in the end, from their own feelings of self-worth.

But the Langton tragedy? That was the remaining unfinished business. She'd been right that Robert's mania was decades old. But now she knew he couldn't have done it, who did that leave? The traveling man who'd passed through town without leaving a mark and buried the body far away? Or could it have been someone who'd lived in Lithgow at the time, killed Shelagh, and dumped her body far enough away not to be found, before leaving town months or even years later when his move wouldn't arouse suspicion? After all, that's what a sane man who valued his freedom would do, whether he'd killed her accidentally or not.

Both these options had been in her mind throughout

the past weeks, and she'd pushed them away, unwilling to accept she'd never solve this mystery. Her own self-worth was on the line here. She'd been so successful with mysteries up until now, she felt it was impossible she'd been called to this mystery if there wasn't a solution. That only left someone in town who had been responsible for the events and yet felt secure enough to stay. Why? There were only two men she knew of who fitted that description. And she was to be with both of them tonight.

33

A KNOWING GLANCE

NEXT DAY, after work, as they'd planned, Pauline drove to Steve's house. He jumped into her car and said, "I'm glad you're on time. Drummond called me earlier and asked if we could be at his house by six-thirty because he has somewhere to be later. I said we would."

"Now I want to know where he's going," Pauline said, laughing in what she hoped was a natural way.

"We can't track his every move," Steve said, grinning, "but we can ask."

They didn't need to ask for when he met them at the door, Drummond told them he had a social engagement that had come up just that afternoon.

"Then we won't keep you too long," Pauline said. "I'm afraid it is sheer curiosity on my part. We drove past a few days ago and I was taken by your beautiful home."

"No problem, Miss Riddell," Drummond said, beaming. "I enjoy showing people over the house and gardens. I've put my heart and soul into this place and I'm happy that others want to share it too. Should we start with the house?"

Pauline agreed and he led them through the open-plan

rooms, each furnished in a different theme. Western, in keeping with the exterior, for the main room, but eastern in most of the others.

"You clearly admire a number of Asian cultures," Pauline said. "Arabic in the earlier room and now Japanese."

'I do," he said. "They have kept the long-term, holistic view of life that we in the west have lost," he said. "I meditate every day and practice Tai Chi also."

"Here?" Pauline said, looking around the Japanese room.

"No," he said. "I made the very first place I built on the property into my studio. I see it as kind of like... celebrating my own roots. If you follow me."

Pauline smiled. "I do. It's important to maintain your roots, I feel. Can we see the studio?"

"Well," he said guardedly, "it's a few minutes' walk across the property. If we've time to get there and back before I have to throw you out." He smiled to show he was joking about ejecting them.

As the tour was ending, Pauline asked again, "Do we have time to visit your studio? I've a small yoga studio in my home but I feel yours will provide me with a lot of inspiration to do better."

Drummond checked his watch and nodded. "A quick visit, which is all you'll need for it's much more minimalist than the house."

Despite saying they had little time, Pauline noted he didn't rush them across the open ground to the small stand of eucalyptus trees that surrounded the cabin.

"Did you plant the trees?" she asked. "They give such an air of peace and serenity to the studio." One even had a sleeping koala on a branch, silhouetted against the evening sky.

He shook his head. "I cleared a space among the trees

for my home," he said, "and, of course, I cleared more of the property as I grew into the space. Those trees, and the ones shading the main house, are all that's left of the original bush."

"It must have taken you years of work," Pauline said, "or did you get help?"

He laughed. "When I was clearing the land at the start, I couldn't afford help, and yes it took me years."

"I can imagine," Pauline replied. "It's a big property."

"It was smaller when I began," he said. "I've added to it on all sides to make it what you see today. I value my privacy, you see."

He stopped fifty feet short of the small, rustic cabin to let them look at it set among the gum trees, with a border of flowering shrubs each side of the door. It really was a restful spot.

"I imagine you meditate outside at this time of year," Pauline said. "It must be very hot inside such a small cabin."

Drummond nodded. "That's true," he said. "Behind the cabin is a small terrace that I use for my summer meditations. Though it isn't just the heat. I love the outdoors so I'm only inside in winter."

Pauline turned to face him and asked, "Have we time to see your terrace?"

Their eyes met. He held her gaze steadily and said, "Perhaps, another time. I really do have an important appointment."

Pauline smiled. "I'd like that," she said. "I'm sure I'd learn a lot from seeing the place close up. Just seeing what you've done here gives me such ideas."

He escorted them back to the house and waved them goodbye before hurrying inside as they drove away.

"I kept quiet," Steve said. "I didn't want to steer the

conversation away from where you wanted it to go. Did you learn anything from this visit?"

"I learned everything I wanted to learn," Pauline said. "Unfortunately, I think he did too."

Steve frowned. "Such as?"

"If I'm right," Pauline said. "He'll be leaving on a trip very soon. Could you keep a watch on the property for the next few days?"

"Where might he be going?" Steve asked.

"I don't know," Pauline said. "Just out of the country for a start."

"Are you saying he's involved in the unpleasant things that have been happening to you, or the Langton tragedy?"

"It might be both," Pauline said. "He has a lot to lose if our new procedures cut him off from our company payments, which I think they will."

"Why not have the police watch him?"

"I'm going to alert them," Pauline said. "However, I know their answer will be that they aren't staffed to provide round-the-clock surveillance."

"You think he has stuff stashed in that cabin and he'll want to move it before we visit again?"

"I think he'll want to be abroad long before we visit again," Pauline said.

"Okay, I'll watch," Steve said. "You'll have to do the evening shift. I still have a life, you know."

"I'll take over around six o'clock," Pauline said. "Then you can get away for a few hours."

"Is it wise for you to be alone here for so long," Steve asked. "I could be back quite quickly."

"You need to do your stuff and be back for the night shift," Pauline said.

"What?"

"It has to be twenty-four hours," Pauline said.

"Wait," Steve cried. "We don't need to watch at all. We can have the local travel agent tell us when he buys a ticket."

Pauline shook her head. "He'll buy a ticket at Sydney Airport and not before."

"Like that other guy did last year."

"Exactly. He won't want any early warning of his trip to become local knowledge," Pauline said.

"When do we start?"

"Tomorrow," Pauline replied. "He'll have some preparations to make before he goes. I judge he'll be packing tomorrow. With luck, we'll see the car being loaded."

34

A STAKEOUT

AFTER WORK THE FOLLOWING EVENING, Pauline dressed in warmer clothes, for here in the mountains with autumn coming on, it was growing chilly when the sun went down. She threw blankets in the back of the car, drove out to Drummond's place to find Steve and give him a break. It took some time to find him, for he'd hidden himself and his car in a mess of intertwined wattle bushes. She parked her own car out of sight of the house and walked to his.

"Anything?" she asked.

"Nothing," Steve said. "He's been back and forth during the day but seems to be settled for the night now."

"He's in there?" Pauline asked.

"Yes. His car is around the back so unless he went out over the field back there, he's still at home."

"There are no lights on?"

"It's early," Steve said. "When the sun goes down, there'll be lights."

Pauline knew he was right, but the thought that Drummond had already given them the slip made her anxious.

"When you go," she said, "drive around that side of the property and just confirm his car is still there, please."

"Sure," he said, "but it won't mean much. If he's run already, he must have left his car, crossed the field, walked back into town to pick up another one, and driven off in that. He'll be long gone by now. It's two hours since he went in there."

"You aren't making me feel any better," Pauline said.

"I'll be back about midnight," Steve said, "and you can go home and sleep."

"You're sure this is okay for you?" Pauline asked. "It's a lot of hours."

"I'm an old newshound," Steve said, grinning. "I cut my teeth on days like this."

Pauline got out of his car; he backed it out of the thicket and drove away. She returned to her own car and edged it into the gap Steve's car had made in the undergrowth. Adjusting her binoculars to observe the house in detail, Pauline settled down to wait. As the sun sank behind the mountains, kangaroos appeared out of the bush for their evening meal. The koala was still sleeping in the tree, she noted, now a lonely silhouette against a fiery red sky.

True to his word, Steve arrived at midnight, and they exchanged places. She backed her own car onto the narrow trail behind the thicket so Steve could edge his into their lookout position.

"His car was still there?" Pauline asked as they took a few moments to chat.

Steve nodded. "Yeah, and as you see, the lights are on inside."

"They are and I even see movement sometimes," Pauline said. "Anyway, it's all yours. Be sure to come by my house if you see he's running. Otherwise, I'll be back at dawn to give you another break."

There had been no change when Pauline arrived at dawn, and Steve drove off for a shower and breakfast. And nothing had changed when he returned two hours later.

"I'll be back this evening at five," Pauline said. "I'll leave work early. My being there right now isn't helping much anyway."

35

CAR CHASE, CAR CRASH

PAULINE ARRIVED BEFORE FIVE, as promised, and Steve took off. There'd been plenty of activity throughout the day, Steve told her before he left, but nothing yet suggested a final dash.

Pauline wondered if she'd misunderstood everything and began going through the visit she and Steve had made to Drummond's place. It had all seemed innocent enough until that last moment when their eyes met. Had she got it wrong? After all, he was a man who was famously awkward around women. Was that all she'd seen in his gaze? His awkwardness?

Suddenly, as the light was fading, she saw a shadow illuminated in the external house lights moving across the wall of an outbuilding. She trained her binoculars on the shadow. Was it wishful thinking or was the shadow carrying bags from the house to the car? She decided the shadow was carrying bags and watched the loading continue. This was more than a vacation. Now she needed to get to the police station or the nearby phone box. She'd found the phone box on the first day of their surveillance for just this reason. She backed up the car and drove quickly away. It would have to be the phone box because even the few extra minutes to get into town could be disastrous.

"Sergeant," she said, when the phone was answered. "You have to get word out to stop Mr. Drummond. He's leaving the country and you need to talk to him about the Langton murders."

"We will need some actual evidence before we can stop him leaving anywhere, Miss Riddell," the desk sergeant said.

"I'll tell you where you'll find evidence when you have him in custody," Pauline said. "Tell Inspector Halleck to get a call out to all the police stations between here and Sydney and at the airport."

As she spoke, she saw the lights of his car making its way to the highway.

"I have to go. He's on the move," she said. "I'm going to follow him."

'Now..." the sergeant began but Pauline didn't wait to hear what it was she shouldn't do. She hung up and, hiding her face until Drummond's car passed, raced out to her own car and set off in pursuit.

She was already a few minutes behind, and he was out of sight before she was moving, but he wasn't hard to find. There were few cars on the road. Everyone was home having their evening meal, and she'd been sure he'd take the road to Sydney. She was right.

As they climbed out of Lithgow on the road through the mountains, Pauline noticed the speed of his car was picking up. Either he was worried about missing his flight, the possibility of being pursued was making him nervous, or he'd spotted her tailing him. She pressed the accelerator to maintain a distance between them that she hoped would prevent him recognizing her car, but a distance where she wouldn't lose sight of him for more than a few seconds when his car disappeared around corners.

His speed continued increasing and she found it hard to keep him in sight with the twists and turns in the road. She decided she had to close the gap and accelerated. His car increased its speed further and they were now doing over eighty miles per hour along a narrow twisting mountain road. It wasn't safe but she was determined not to lose him. If nothing else, she needed to know where he was flying to. The police could ask for extradition from wherever it was.

A sudden straight section near the top of the plateau allowed him to accelerate again and, before Pauline could react, a police car, waiting in a hidden spot at the side of the road, set its light and horn flashing. It pulled out to give chase. Pauline smiled and slowed quickly. Maybe luck was on her side, after all. Even if they just held him for speeding and dangerous driving, it might give her time to get Lithgow's finest to the scene.

As the road began to descend back toward the valley floor, she had a good view of the two cars racing down the side of the mountain. Whatever speed they were doing now was insane, she thought momentarily before her thoughts were overtaken by events. Drummond's white Holden ran straight off the road, hitting a barrier that should have kept it from falling but didn't. The car flipped, its tail somersaulting over its nose which was buried deep in the barrier. Then the whole car, doors and other broken pieces flying off, plummeted down, down, down before smashing into the trees below. She thought there'd be an explosion like in the movies but there wasn't. The car just vanished into the bush. The police car slithered to a halt near the broken barrier and the two policemen from the car leapt out, staring over the edge in shock.

That's the end of that, Pauline thought, as she slowed her car and stopped behind the police cruiser. There'd be no need for a trial now. No one could survive that drop.

One of the two officers came to her car. "Stay in your vehicle," he said. "It's not safe to be outside here."

"I saw what happened," Pauline said, "from the top of the hill."

"Then we'll need to take a statement from you," the officer said, "but not here. If you can give us your name and address, we'll do it later."

Pauline handed over her driver's license and provided her phone number and address. When he'd finished noting the details in his notebook, he said, "Are you okay to drive? You've probably had a nasty shock."

"I'm fine," Pauline said, and she was.

"Then drive carefully," he said. "These roads can surprise unwary drivers and, however you think you feel, you have just witnessed a horrific event. Don't underestimate how that can disturb you."

Pauline assured him she would be the most careful driver in New South Wales for the rest of her day and slowly pulled onto the road, heading back to Lithgow.

36

MISS RIDDELL REVEALS ALL

"This is Miss Riddell's story to tell," Inspector Halleck said to the group of interested parties sitting together in Pauline's living room. "All I can do here is tell you what we found where Miss Riddell suggested we look." He paused and then, addressing Pauline, asked, "Would you care to give the background?"

"I can do that after," Pauline said, "I think it would be kindest to confirm the truth quickly, particularly for Mrs. Langton, Mrs. Brown and Eve's sake." She doubted Eve would care; it had been hard enough to persuade her to attend. But it was just possible her reluctance was for fear of the pain she might feel.

"Very well," Inspector Halleck said, nodding, "I'll be brief. Acting on information given to us by Miss Riddell, we removed the terrace behind Mr. Drummond's old cabin. There we found the remains of a woman that have now been clearly identified by our pathologist as being those of Shelagh Langton. While this must be a painful discovery for you, Mrs. Brown and Miss Langton, I hope this will in time bring some measure of comfort to you."

"When can we bury her decently, Inspector?" Mrs. Brown asked quietly.

"There will be an inquest but at this stage I think it will be little more than a formality so very soon, I should say." There were no additional questions and he turned again to Pauline, saying, "I shall leave you to explain further." He bade them good day and left them.

"I think you always suspected Drummond, didn't you?" Steve asked, not waiting for Pauline to gather her thoughts.

"I did," Pauline said. "Yes."

"Why?" Mrs. Langton asked. "He was always good to us during that time, unlike so many."

"He reminded me of someone back home. A man called Sid Potter," Pauline said. "I don't mean to look at, although even in that there was something. Potter was also a small-town businessman and very successful in his way, but you always had to count your change whenever you bought something from him."

Mrs. Brown smiled grimly. "That's all of them in *business*," she said, pronouncing business with real venom.

Pauline smiled. "That's true but this was more than just sharp practice. It showed in other ways. Particularly in his dealings with women. I don't mean he was violent. He was obsessive, and that's how it turned out to be."

"Did he murder someone?" Steve asked.

"No, he didn't," Pauline said, "or at least not that I know of. What brought him to mind was, like Drummond, he was successful in business right away. Anyway, Sid Potter bought a car on a hire-purchase agreement. That's a wicked financial scheme in my opinion but still popular today. I'm sure you had or have something like it here.

"I digress. The car he bought was one of those open-topped two-seater sports cars, so low you could trip over it if you weren't careful, and with a fabric cover for when it rained. Most unsuitable in the climate of northern England." She paused, shaking her head disapprovingly.

"Yes?" the others spoke almost with one voice.

"Oh, yes," Pauline said, brought back to the present by their eagerness. "Well, Potter loved that car with a passion he showed to nothing else. Polishing it and buying it presents. You know the sort of thing, extra lights and accessories, silly things. Then business turned bad." She paused briefly before continuing, "We wondered how he would keep up the payments and many were genuinely sorry for the heartbreak he'd suffer when the car would have to go back to the dealer."

"He destroyed it?" Steve suggested.

"I'm sure he did," Pauline said, "but no one can be certain. He claimed to have slid off the road because of wet fallen leaves. The car hit a tree, he scrambled out just in time before it caught fire, and, yes, the car was destroyed. I'm sure the insurance was suspicious but, in the end, they paid, and all was well."

"Was he heartbroken?" Mrs. Langton asked.

"He said so, but I never felt that he was," Pauline said. "I think he was content because if he couldn't have it, no one else could and that was enough to calm his spirit. At least, that's what I thought at the time."

Mrs. Langton shuddered. "Has he murdered anyone; do you think?"

Pauline said, "I don't know. He was certainly capable of doing so and, after all, Drummond successfully kept Shelagh's body hidden for twenty years. Maybe the man Drummond reminded me of is doing the same."

The others stared at her. "You don't think..." Mrs. Langton began.

Pauline shook her head. "No, I don't think he is," she said. "I'm just saying it's possible. He is that kind of person. Anyway, I don't live near him anymore, so I'll never know."

"What made you certain enough to go to the police?" Steve asked.

Pauline pondered whether to tell them that when she set out that night to view Drummond's house, she was still wavering between Steve Larsen or Fergus Drummond as the most likely killer. She thought it best not to.

"When Drummond showed us around his property," Pauline said. "He hesitated when I asked to see his original cabin. His answers were evasive, and it made me think again of Potter's unwillingness to share something so precious. Finally, however, as we looked at it, his expression when I turned to him and our eyes met, convinced me. And he saw it in my eyes, I was sure. He knew I knew, and I knew he would run. After all, he couldn't kill both Steve and me."

"And you think he persuaded Bruce to kill himself?" Mrs. Langton asked. "That's what the police said."

"I think he did," Pauline said. "But we'll never know for sure now. I think he used his friendship to push Bruce over the edge. He was a clever, manipulative man who could make sympathy a weapon. Bruce was already certain he was to blame for Shelagh's disappearance, whether it was murder by someone or just by abandoning her when she most needed his support. Drummond would have repeatedly assured him that no one blamed him and then, when he judged the moment was right, he asked 'just tell us where she's buried, Bruce'. Those words would be like a knife in the heart to Bruce and from a man he'd thought was his only remaining friend."

"You've lifted a weight off my life, Miss Riddell," Mrs. Brown said. "I've blamed myself for so long because I felt exactly like that. I thought it was my lack of support that had driven Shelagh away."

"We all do things we later regret," Pauline said. "None of us is innocent of that." She smiled but felt it wouldn't do to entirely absolve any of her audience, for each in their own way had all let Shelagh and Bruce down.

"I wish my husband could have been here today," Mrs. Langton said, sadly. "The inspector is right. There is some comfort in knowing Bruce didn't kill Shelagh, though my heart aches for him, now I know for sure his final despair."

Mrs. Brown said, hesitantly, "I know that if my husband could be with us, he'd want me to tell you how sorry I am that I've believed badly of Bruce all these years. I'm afraid I've always believed he was guilty, and in a way, you were too for being his mother." She held out her hand and Mrs. Langton took it.

"That man robbed us both of our children," she said. "Together, with Steve's help, we can change the old story for a new, truer one."

"Will you help, Eve?" Mrs. Brown asked.

Eve Langton, who had sat silently throughout the whole event, nodded.

Perhaps knowing she'd been the lover of the man who'd murdered her mother and led to the death of her father might be enough to bring her to her senses before she went too far along the bleak path she was traveling. Pauline hoped so, anyway.

"What's next for you?" Steve said, when a silence had fallen over the group.

"Home," Pauline said. "I've done what I was brought here to do, and my services will no longer be required. And, while I love your sunburned Australia, I find it too hot for my English constitution. I look forward to rain.

Without rain, you know, there's no green and pleasant land."

One week later, with her role at the factory filled by Andy MacDowell, Pauline walked through the now repaired old house for one last time. It was quiet. No voices whispered as she moved through the rooms and, as she entered the bathroom, no chill made the hair on her forearms rise.

"Goodbye," she said to the empty room. "I pray you're at peace now."

She returned to the hallway as the driver knocked on the door. She opened it and, after a cheery good morning, the driver took her bags to the car. Pauline looked back into the dark hall. There was no one there. There never had been. It was just her imagination. What else could it have been? There are no such things as ghosts.

Her boss got out of the car, "I hope you don't mind me escorting you," he called.

"Not at all," Pauline said, smiling. "We out-of-work people need to stick together."

He smiled. "New challenges await us, Pauline," he said. "That's the way to look at it. Now, stop dithering and let's go."

Realizing she was still at the door and strangely reluctant to close it, Pauline swiftly pulled the door shut and pushed the keys through the mail flap.

"I came for the ride," her boss said, "and because I heard that not only were you reforming the company's financial procedures, but you'd also found time to solve a decades-old murder. What was that all about?"

Pauline thought quickly. He would want to know why she began, and she might need a recommendation from him someday. Would he do that if he thought she was mad? It was probably best to play the beginning down.

She said at last, "I discovered the house I was renting was the site of a suicide years before and the wife of the man who killed himself had disappeared just before he did it. I'm a local history enthusiast and it started me researching in my off hours."

"And that led you to a murder?"

"Yes," she said. "The more I learned the surer I became that a great injustice had been done."

"But lots of old houses must have similarly sad stories locked in them," her boss said, perplexed. "Why did you think this was about injustice?"

Pauline paused. She couldn't explain properly without mentioning her experience. How badly did she need a reference letter?

Finally, she said, "you will find what I'm about to tell you impossible to believe. I do myself."

"That doesn't make sense."

"Then listen," she said and related as accurately as she could the voices and the chilling presence in the bathroom.

"You don't believe in ghosts, surely? Not a sensible, logical woman such as you?"

"I don't believe in ghosts, no," Pauline said, "but I've come to accept there's more around us than we can see."

"You'll have to explain that," her boss said.

"Well, I believe in God, and I can't see God," Pauline said.

"That's just belief," he said, "not evidence. I would expect better from a sleuth."

"It's true, I'm just a humble believer in an Almighty, but take the great scientists," Pauline said. "Leaving aside whether they believe in God or not, many believe there's such a thing as dark matter, which is everywhere, all around us, invisible, and can't be experienced in any physical way but is vital for the universe's very existence. And they are logical, reasonable people, I'm sure you'll agree?"

"Your ghosts weren't dark matter though," he objected. "They could be heard and felt by you."

"I was just setting the context for what I'm about to say," Pauline said. "Scientists have also postulated parallel universes, a multiverse, not a universe. Each separated by perhaps tiny degrees of probability."

"I see," he said. "You think sometimes, in some places, two universes come close enough to be seen by the inhabitants of each?"

"I'm not a scientist so I'm not best placed to speak on this but, what if in this case, there was a universe running parallel to ours in which the events of twenty years ago were only now taking place? Or something like that."

"Sounds unlikely to me," he said, "but I wasn't there, and you were, so I'll go along with it."

"I said I didn't believe what happened either," Pauline said. "I can't really explain it except to say it happened, and it convinced me a great wrong had been done. Maybe I just have a feeling for injustice. After all, we understand a talent for so many other things, why not for justice?"

"Why not, indeed," he said. "And you never had any doubts about it being Drummond? You knew right from the start?"

Pauline laughed. "I had lots of doubts," she said. "Until that fateful visit to Drummond's property, I was almost sure it was Steve Larsen, my oh-so-willing helper."

"Why?"

"He hadn't told me he was rumored to have been having an affair with Shelagh," Pauline said. "I heard that from someone else."

"And was he?'

Pauline shook her head. "He hadn't told me because he had no idea anyone thought that. He hadn't been having an affair, so he had no guilty conscience about it. He was just a single man who someone, probably Drummond, practiced their malice upon."

"Rumors and gossip are horrible things," her boss said, frowning.

"And yet," Pauline replied, "everyone loves both. And I wouldn't solve nearly so many puzzles as I do if it wasn't for rumors and gossip. They're the lifeblood of conversation and also the trail guilty people leave behind them in the social sphere."

37
HOME AND ANOTHER 'NEW WORLD'

"Goodbye, Pauline," her boss said as they shook hands before she went into the departure lounge of Sydney airport. "I'm glad you decided to join me in my rehabilitation of the company. I hope our work will be enough to save it. Some good people work there."

"I was happy to help," Pauline said, "and I also hope they do well, though I fear not."

"You think old dogs can't learn new tricks," he said frowning.

She nodded. "It's hard. In my work, I've seen so many companies who knew what they had to do to save themselves, but I saw it in their behavior and heard it in their words; they couldn't change. Everyone generally remains themselves to the end. And in a way, I admire that. It's honest and, I think, brave."

She turned away and entered the lounge, not looking forward to the next twenty-four hours at all.

"Courage, Pauline," she said softly to herself. "In the past, it would have been a month on a steam ship or three months on a sailing ship and yet people did it all the time."

. . .

"Glad to have you back," her English boss said when she phoned him to let him know when she'd be in the office. "We have a lot on, and we need all hands to the pumps."

"Things have grown worse here in even the short time I've been away," Pauline said. "I heard the news on the radio coming home from the airport. The newspaper headlines were outlandish too."

"Oh, we're heading for one almighty crash all right," her boss said, "but that means lots of firms wanting our advice on how to position themselves for the future. If Margaret Thatcher wins the next election, and it's looking very likely, she'll shake those old cronies out of everywhere. They're all terrified."

"I'll be in tomorrow," Pauline said. "If we have exciting times ahead, I don't want to miss a moment."

He laughed. "I only hope *we* survive," he said. "Who knows what the future will hold."

"The future belongs to those who show up," Pauline said firmly, "and that will be me." She replaced the handset and looked in the hall mirror. Her face was lined with weariness; she looked haggard from the flight, but in her eyes, she saw the fierce light of battle. She'd triumphed in one 'new world' and now she was ready to do the same here in her own.

Author's Closing Note:

In 1977, we were newly married with no children when I was offered the opportunity to work in Australia for six months. We couldn't say no to an offer like that and off we went. We rented a house in Lithgow and moved in. As I was the new kid on the block at work, I was on almost permanent night shifts, which I didn't mind so much because I was young and didn't need too much sleep. It left us plenty of time for exploring the beautiful Blue Mountains of New South Wales every day. It was ideal, except for one hard to explain feature of the house. I first noticed it when I went to take a shower. The moment the shower curtain closed I could feel there was someone just on the other side. It was like the shower scene in the movie *Psycho*, which I hadn't seen but knew of. As well, my wife would go out during the day to let me sleep. Except, I couldn't. The room, the house, was filled with voices. I checked everything. The windows were shut. The doors were shut. I went outside often. I was sure I'd find neighbors talking in their gardens or animals on the roof, but I never did. In fact, there were no voices in this quiet residential area during the day, only the ones inside the house. My problem here was simple. My wife was in the house alone each night and, as she didn't mention hearing voices or sinister presences in the bathroom, I couldn't suggest we move without raising in her mind the same nonsensical imaginings I was experiencing, which would be horribly unfair.

At the end of our time in the house, and Australia, we drove out of Lithgow, and I stopped at a lookout spot where we could see the town laid out before us in the valley below. After a moment, I said, "I've never been so glad to leave a place as I am this one."

"Didn't you like Lithgow?" my wife asked.

"Lithgow is great but that house was haunted, I'm certain. I didn't want to say anything before because you'd have worried about my sanity or been infected with the same nonsense yourself."

"Oh," she said. "I thought it was just me who thought it was haunted."

"The shower was the worst," I said. "In the end, I couldn't draw the curtains. I just mopped up the floor after. Did you hear voices?"

"Almost the moment you left for work every evening they started," she said, "and sometimes they were so loud, even if I fell asleep, they woke me in the night. I looked everywhere for an answer, inside and out, but there was nothing."

We had shared the same peculiar experience but had chosen not to 'share it' because it wouldn't be fair to alarm the other.

These events have stayed with us for over forty years. We aren't psychic or sensitive in any way. We'd lived in many places before Lithgow and have lived in many more places of all kinds after, and we've never had that experience again. Occasionally, when something reminds us, we wonder if the people who've lived in the house since have shared our experience. We'll never know if they have or what caused the noises or the feeling because, unlike Miss Riddell, we didn't really investigate. It did, however, provide a foundation for this fictional mystery story about old murders and their effect on the people who live on after.

Polite Request:

THANK you for reading my book. If you love this book, please, please, please don't forget to leave a review! Every review matters and it matters a lot!

Head over to Amazon (or wherever you purchased this book) to leave a review for me. Here's the link on Amazon:

Miss Riddell's Paranormal Mystery

. . .

I THANK you now and forever :-)

BONUS CONTENT

Here's a peek at the next Miss Riddell mystery: The Girl in the Gazebo: A Miss Riddell Cozy Mystery.

Chapter 1: Muskoka, Ontario, Canada. June 1984

Pauline Riddell gazed from her tenth-floor office window, out across the eastern side of Toronto, toward Scarborough and the outer reaches of the Greater Toronto Area. It was late morning, and the sun was now high in the sky, which made looking out of the window more pleasant for even the sun-dimmed windows couldn't quite blunt the glare of a summer sun in the early morning. She sighed. The final draft of her report was waiting on her desk for her to finish editing but she couldn't settle. It wasn't just the report, though she hated editing and re-editing documents, it was just life. She'd been in Toronto over four years now and she felt the call of Yorkshire more and more with every passing day.

She'd taken this position when it became clear the company she worked for in England wasn't going to survive the upheaval brought about by Prime Minister Margaret

Thatcher's reforms. It seemed to her, watching the news, that very little had survived. Yet, when Pauline returned home for family visits, little seemed to have changed. In fact, far from the dire straits the news reported each night, everyone looked a lot more prosperous. As she'd remarked to her old boss, when they'd met in his favorite pub, 'everyone is now driving Mercedes-Benz cars. How is this the ruin I read so much about?' He laughed and reminded her not to believe anything she read in the news.

Pauline had intended returning home this summer for her vacation and sound out employment opportunities with her ex-colleagues. Only an 'emergency' audit had come up and she'd been given a team and the task of completing it quickly. Now it was done, and the report almost finished, her thoughts again turned toward home.

The phone rang, intruding on her musings, and for a moment she considered letting it ring but she knew Carly, her secretary, would never have passed it through if it hadn't been urgent. Pauline walked to her desk, picked up the handset and said, "Yes?" in a tone she hoped would deter any frivolous caller.

"Pauline," her boss said. "I need you here right away." He sounded distraught, not at all his usual self.

"Where are you?" Pauline asked. He was supposed to be at his cottage up in Muskoka, the region of lakes, forests, and summer homes for the better-off members of Toronto's population to the north of the city. And her boss's cottage, she knew, was even more exclusive than most. He wasn't just her boss, he was the owner of the accounting company that had been started by his grandfather, developed into a wealthy firm by his father, and still doing nicely, even in the miserable business environment of the times.

"At the cottage," he replied, testily, "I told you." He

paused, then added, "My plane is on its way to pick you up. Be ready and at the harbor within the hour."

"I'm just finishing the Griffin Report," Pauline said. "It is supposed to go to the Board tomorrow for final approval."

"Give it to Carson. He can finish it off. I need you here now."

"Why? What's happening?"

"My daughter, Lynette, has been found dead," he said. "They say it's an accident or suicide but it isn't. It can't be. You have some experience in these things. You can get to the bottom of it."

Pauline's heart sank. Trying to overturn what most likely would be an accident or suicide, teenagers were notoriously prone to both, with a distraught father hovering, who was also her boss, would be a nightmare.

"I'll be at the seaplane dock in an hour," Pauline said. "But I can't promise this will turn out the way you want."

"Just get here," her boss said. "You'll see."

ALSO BY P.C. JAMES

In the Beginning, There Was a Murder

Then There Were ... Two Murders?

A Murder for Christmas

Miss Riddell and the Heiress

It's Murder, on a Galapagos Cruise

In The Beginning, There Was a Murder (in Large Print)

AND NOW you can pre-order the next Miss Riddell Cozy Mystery:

The Girl in the Gazebo: A Miss Riddell Amateur Female Sleuth Historical Cozy Mystery

Or visit my P.C. James Amazon Author Page

ABOUT THE AUTHOR

I've always loved mysteries, especially those involving Agatha Christie's Miss Marple. Perhaps because Miss Marple reminded me of my aunts when I was growing up. But Agatha never told us much about Miss Marple's earlier life. While writing my own elderly super-sleuth series, I'm tracing her career from the start. As you'll see, if you follow the Miss Riddell Cozy Mysteries over the coming years.

However, this is my Bio so here goes with all you need to know about me: After retiring, I became a writer and, as a writer, I spend much of my day staring at the computer screen hoping inspiration will strike. I'm pleased to say, it eventually does. For the rest, you'll find me running, cycling, walking, and taking wildlife photos wherever and whenever I can. My cozy mystery series begins in northern England because that was my home growing up and that's also the home of so many great cozy mysteries. Stay with me though because Miss Riddell loves to travel as much as I do and the stories will take us to many different places around the world.

Copyright © 2021 by P.C. James

All rights reserved.

No part of this book may be reproduced in any form or by any electronic or mechanical means, including information storage and retrieval systems, without written permission from the author, except for the use of brief quotations in a book review.

Miss Riddell's Paranormal Mystery©

PC James Copyright notice: All rights reserved under the International and Pan-American Copyright Conventions. No part of this book may be reproduced or transmitted in any form or by any means, electronic or mechanical, including photocopying and recording, or by any information storage and retrieval system, without permission in writing from publisher.

Miss Riddell's Paranormal Mystery is a work of fiction. Names, places, characters, and incidents are either the product of the author's imagination or are used fictitiously, and any resemblance to any actual persons, living or dead, organizations, events, or locales is entirely coincidental.

Warning: the unauthorized reproduction or distribution of this copyrighted work is illegal. Criminal copyright infringement, including infringement without monetary gain, is investigated by the FBI and is punishable by up to 5 years in prison and a fine of $250,000.

For more information: email: pj4429358@gmail.com

❦ Created with Vellum

Printed in Great Britain
by Amazon